SKID ROW

A Novel

Praise for *SKID ROW*

"Joe Werner's vivid and moving memories of Depression era
Memphis shine new light on a community too often seen in
literature as one dimensional. In his "Skid Row" neighborhood,
black and white, Jew and Christian, coexist, barely surviving,
in a world of almost insurmountable hardship and danger.
But his memorable characters have a hopeful sweetness,
regardless of their very real flaws, revealing the goodness
Werner has found even in the roughest personalities."
—Bridget Smith Pieschel, Professor of English,
Mississippi University for Women

"Tinners and bums ... high-steppers and real lookers ... "stew
heads" and fly-by-nights. This is Skid Row in Memphis in the 1930s,
and *Skid Row* is Joe Werner's fictionalized portrait of growing up
there, a teenager during the Depression at work among the roofers
in his father's sheet-metal shop. It's a vanished world that Werner
describes, but in these pages, it's brought vividly back to life
with honesty, some humor—and heart."
—Leonard Gill, *Memphis Flyer*

"Tender and vivid portrayal of the "tinners" and other characters
on the street. I found many of the stories ... about Uncle Louis,
Otis and Sweeney, and the others quite moving."
—Amy Williams, Literary Agent, McCormick & Williams

SKID ROW

A Novel

Joe Werner

SUNSTONE
PRESS

SANTA FE

Sunstone books may be purchased for educational, business, or sales promotional use. For information please write: Special Markets Department, Sunstone Press, P.O. Box 2321, Santa Fe, New Mexico 87504-2321.

Book and Cover design • Vicki Ahl
Body typeface • Trebuchet MS
Printed on acid free paper

Library of Congress Cataloging-in-Publication Data

Werner, Joseph H., 1930-
    Skid row : a novel / by Joseph H. Werner, Jr.
        p. cm.
    ISBN 978-0-86534-802-8 (softcover : alk. paper)
    1. Skid row--Fiction. 2. Working poor--Fiction. 3. People with social disabilities--Fiction. 4. Depressions--1929--Fiction. 5. Memphis (Tenn.)--Fiction. I. Title.
    PS3623.E7657S55 2011
    813'.6--dc22
                                2011000630

WWW.SUNSTONEPRESS.COM
SUNSTONE PRESS / POST OFFICE BOX 2321 / SANTA FE, NM 87504-2321 /USA
(505) 988-4418 / ORDERS ONLY (800) 243-5644 / FAX (505) 988-1025

To my loving wife Amelia, the one who
encouraged me to write this book and
to never give up.

A special thanks to Kim Kimbrough, my writer
friend who prodded me to finish *Skid Row*.

Don't go around saying the world owes you a living.
The world owes you nothing. It was here first.

—Mark Twain

1

Hard Times On Skid Row

The bum that put the touch on me was a wobbly little guy, red-eyed and pasty-faced, hands trembling like leaves on a birch tree in a strong wind. He wore pants much too large for his skinny waist; the cuffs turned up but still dragging the ground, a shirt that was once white, now smudged with dirt and remnants of old food. His worn out shoes had no laces, the tongues flapped and the loose soles made a slapping noise with each step.

In a high-pitched voice that shook so badly he could hardly get the words out he said, "Boss, you got a quarter so I can get some food? I ain't et for two days."

After I gave Andy a quarter, knowing damned well he was headed for the closest beer joint, I flipped the butt of the cigarette I had been smoking into a nearby gutter, straightened up from my lean on the door jamb, went back into my tiny office, the one with sheetrock walls painted a sickly lime green, and sat behind my artificial walnut desk.

I worked in a sheet metal shop owned and operated by my dad and blind uncle on a section of Poplar Avenue near downtown Memphis, an area for the years during the Depression known as Skid Row. The buildings stretched along six blocks or so of a half tarmac street scattered with potholes and gullies. They were tall, musty and tattered things leaning against one another shrouded in smoky red brick seemingly untouched by the sun. Most were two-story with parapets extending far above the tar and gravel roofs where tiny saplings grew from the old mortared joints as if trying to breathe life into the dark street below.

It was an area filled with sadness, desperation and at times, violence. It was also a place of darkness and silence. It was the place that I spent most of my life as a lad and young man and one that has long since been forgotten.

2

Jew Bill Ain't Dead, He's Just Drunk

Shorty and I saw the whole thing from across the street. The two of us had just put in eight long hours in the blazing heat of a Memphis July working on a tar and gravel roof. Shorty was angling toward the curb, parking the sputtering pick-up in front of Dad and Uncle Louis's sheet metal shop when he saw Jew Bill fall out of his chair.

Shorty, a shaky driver at his best of times yelled, "Look over yonder JoJo! Jew Bill done kilt hisself. I knew whiskey was gonna get that ole man one of these days."

I was only fourteen, just starting high school at the Brothers but I knew a drunk when I saw one, and my first thought was hell, Jew Bill ain't dead, he's just passed out.

Shorty sat there jittery, hand-holding the steering wheel as I jumped out of the old Dodge and ran across the street to where Jew Bill was reclining in a half prone position snoring up a storm. A few bums were clustered around him in a circle shuffling their feet, staring in curiosity, wondering if there might be a sip left in the whiskey bottle protruding from Jew Bill's back pocket.

A tinner by the name of Fingers came out of the place, grabbed the half conscious Bill by the scruff of the neck, and stiff-walked him into the sheet metal shop, the one owned by Bill's brother Abe Chlem, a short, bald-headed little fellow.

As he walked Jew Bill into the shop, Fingers turned a dirty, crooked index appendage at me and said, "Get your ass back across the street to your old man's shop, boy. You ain't got no business here."

I was the one who generally helped Bill when he was in this shape and being nosey as hell to boot, all I was trying to do was get a look into that abyss the Jewish brothers called a tinsmith shop but standing in the sunlight, my vision penetrated only five feet or so into the shadows.

Following Fingers and Bill at a safe distance, I stepped into the shop where the darkness enveloped me and as I did, I felt as if I were walking back in time. The shop was only about thirty feet wide with tongue and groove hardwood flooring, a ceiling so high it disappeared into obscurity, and lights that hung from extension cords with bulbs surrounded by shop-made metal reflectors.

The shop was so narrow that when a tinner needed to turn a length of gutter or flashing, his fellow worker learned to watch carefully as the metal dodged the wall, the light, and his head. I backed out while Fingers helped Bill into a chair then I ran across the street where Shorty stood.

"He ain't hurt none Shorty. He's just drunk again," I said.

Since all the commotion was over, Shorty took the pint of whiskey he had hidden under the driver's seat and trotted into Dad's shop where the crew stood waiting impatiently for their afternoon nip. I followed Shorty into the concrete block building with the name Werner Sheet Metal Works splashed in bright red letters across the dirt-splattered plate glass window.

At the death of my grandfather who had owned the shop next door to Chlem's, Dad and Uncle Louis had built a new building, an inexpensive structure directly across the street from Chlem

Sheet Metal Company, a simple building with no frills and a small office just big enough for a desk and two chairs. The sheetrock walls were painted a vomit-colored lime green selected by my sister, an aspiring artist who insisted the correct name for the color to be chartreuse. Next to the plate glass window was an overhead door that opened into a shop filled with brakes for bending metal, benches for the men to work on, and racks to hold the steel. The whole affair was as unpretentious as the men who owned the business and the men who worked for them. Since the building was completed just as the Depression years of the 1930s hit us like a sledgehammer, there seemed to be small chance that the company could survive. However, through hardheaded German stubbornness, lots of work, and the luck of a huge hailstorm, my dad and uncle kept the place afloat.

3

The Melting Pot

Everything necessary for a person to live was right there on Skid Row in that tight little area. A shoe shop, butcher shop, all night café, two sheet metal shops facing one another, and next to Dad and Uncle Louis's sheet metal shop was a two-storied apartment building filled with prostitutes.

Around the corner from our sheet metal shop was a three-storied flophouse with four rooms per floor and a bath at the end of the corridor on each floor. The old geezer who owned the place and lived in one of the prime rooms on the first floor, the one closest to the bath, rented out the other rooms by the hour, a convenience for the corner whores who used it mostly late in the afternoon and into all hours of the night. The young black girls considered it a landfall, a room right across the street even if the bed did creak and the sheets were dirty, that is, if the old geezer had been sober enough that day to put the much used sheets back on the bed.

The guys who lived on Skid Row were barely making it, grabbing any job that would pay a buck. They rented the other rooms not used by the whores, spending most of their time in old chairs on the building's dilapidated porch or on the much used sofa, bent like a swaybacked horse. They drank beer and debated possible solutions to the Depression, and the shape and size, especially the rear end, of the young black whores lolling on the opposite corner.

The street was a melting pot: Greeks, Jews, Germans, Italians, and Poles. They were all part of the makeup, all trying to eke out a living and I was there as a boy and young man to be part of the whole thing, even Uncle Louis and Dad who were constantly at odds with one another about the tinsmith business, among other things, like an old couple that spent too many hours together.

Every day Monday through Friday, ten hours a day, they argued, hollered actually about small things or large, but they always agreed about one thing: Chlem Sheet Metal was doing more business than Werner Sheet Metal, something that made no sense.

Louis leaned against the doorjamb, batted his eyes furiously as if he could see staring across the street at Jew Bill lounging in his chair and saying to me, as if I had the answer, "JoJo, I don't get it. Jews are supposed to own tailor shops or scrap yards, not sheet metal companies."

It was true and Dad had probably hit the nail on the head when he said, "Hell, you know as well as me, Jews always stick together. Abe's just getting while the getting's good. I don't blame him one bit."

Abe was a good guy. Everyone on Skid Row knew it, but no one knew anything about him. He had come up living in a shotgun house, little more than a shack, his father having been killed by a runaway horse when he was a small child. Abe's mother, a domineering type, owned a small sundry store and she, along with Abe and his lazy no account brother Bill, lived in a tiny apartment above the store.

Abe went to a school in a Jewish neighborhood called the Pinch District, an area on north main street where the trolley made a loop and where all the kids waited, jumping on the rear for a free ride downtown. Abe was a roly-poly little guy, slow of foot not fast enough to catch the back of the trolley, his buddies leaving him behind, laughing and waving as they went. And he was the first to have his nose rubbed in the dirt when a kid wanted to steal his lunch, but that didn't matter much. The cheese and crackers weren't very filling anyway. And Abe was always the smallest one in the class. As he would say later, "You know the kind, the kid who always knelt in front when a class picture was taken."

Abe was tough and smart, and after finishing high school, a rarity for kids in the Pinch, Abe went to work for a guy in the scrap iron business, a guy with no children who treated Abe like a sorry stepson. The man was tight as a tick, had no family that he spoke to. His wife was dead and his two sisters refused to speak his name in their houses unless someone called him that old son-of-a-bitch. At his death, he left a large estate to Abe, something that surprised Abe as much as it did the old man's sisters, but certainly not to be refused. And just maybe, that was part of the reason for Abe's kindness.

Abe was still a young man when he saw no future in the scrap metal business, and although not a drinking man himself, he saw a good, safe investment in a Liquor store and with that, he quickly sold the scrap business and bought a liquor store, one near downtown where the lawyers, judges, and court house people shopped, then another near Central Gardens, an affluent neighborhood in midtown. When asked, Abe could never remember how in the hell he had ended up in the sheet metal business. At times it seemed to have come from a thought that his mother brought up, something about his brother Bill needing an occupation but instead, eroded into Jew Bill being a permanent fixture on the sidewalk in his caned-back chair, and a damned sheet metal outfit that never made money, probably lost some, if anyone had kept track.

Of course Dad didn't mention the fact that we were Catholic

and that he went to all the functions put on by the Knights of Columbus where he had a few drinks with the priests and higher ups in the Church. Or how the Brothers ended up with the tile roof and copper metalwork was on all the new Catholic schools and churches. No matter, even with the Depression, Abe had enough work to keep eight or ten men busy, many more than the six or so working at Werner's for less than full time. And he did so without knowing a damned thing about sheet metal, something that really pissed Uncle Louis off.

Abe was rarely at his shop, more than likely spending his time at one of the two liquor stores he owned while Fingers ran the shop, the same guy who got my under my skin, picking on me every chance he got just because I was the boss's son.

Fingers was a big guy, and probably would have been nice looking if he hadn't had a birthmark that covered the right half of his face. He was a bruiser, no doubt about it, with wide shoulders, huge hands, and a face that was ugly as homemade sin.

Some of Dad's men said he was a member of the KKK, and some said hell naw, that he was a damned Nazi. But whatever he was, I tried to stay clear of him. I knew he had a really good-looking wife, one that all the men stared at when she came around and they snickered behind Fingers back telling about a blond-headed kid just out of the Navy, a cousin of Fingers who was screwing her. It seemed that Fingers brought the kid home, figured he could help out down at Chlem's Shop and pay a little rent, but the kid had turned into a good hand and, as the other tinners called it, every time Fingers left the house, his wife was all over that boy.

No one saw me. I was too young to attract any attention but I was nosy as hell, and after seeing that good looking woman, I thought to myself, I don't know if it's true or not, but if I was as ugly and bad tempered as Fingers, I figure I would be watching my back.

If Abe didn't have enough problems with Fingers, he had his brother, known to all of Skid Row as Jew Bill. Bill had two jobs: One was to keep the bums from pestering the men in the shop. At a little over five feet tall and one hundred and twenty pounds, that might have been a chore but the stumblebums Jew Bill bullied were in worse shape than he. The only other job was to answer the telephone.

But Bill had issues. He drank too much, making him drowsy, which meant that when the telephone rang, somewhat of a rarity, it was his job to answer and take a note for Abe, a simple enough request, but often he would think the telephone ringing was a dream and by the time Bill gathered himself and staggered into the little cubby hole Abe used as an office, the caller would have given up in disgust.

Lately, after missing a number of calls and catching hell from Abe, Bill had broached him the idea with of getting an extension for the telephone so that he could sit the instrument on the sidewalk next to his chair where he kept a dirty old legal pad and a stub-nosed pencil. The other issue was how to deal with his brother; that is, if Abe found out that Bill was selling metal to cash paying customers. If someone stopped in front of the shop to purchase a piece of metal, Jew Bill would perk up, straighten the chair, square his hat and state the price of one dollar and twelve cents no matter the size or gauge, but exactly the cost of a pint of Jim Beam. It seemed only a fair trade as far as Bill was concerned, since Abe paid him very little, though he was furnished a cold water flat to live in directly above the shop.

4

Fingers Done Kilt Swede

When the weather turned cold, a bitter bone chilling type of cold with a wind that whipped between the old buildings, it left the brick walls that were already covered in dust with tiny bits of sleet and there would be a silence, a feeling of apprehension and fear on Skid Row.

The down-and-outers—the bums—hell, even the winos would disappear. No one knew where. They would just vanish, most likely finding a warm spot in a deserted basement or under one of the trestle bridges downtown. The only noise that could be heard above the howling wind came from the two sheet metal shops as the men fabricated fittings, banging on metal anvils attached to the walls of the structure, a racket that echoed between the buildings heard only by the beer drinkers in Nick's Café and the bums awakened from their stupor, those lucky enough to be high on canned heat or cheap booze.

Dad was out calling on contractors, driving away from the shop early one morning in his old Plymouth hoping to drum up work. Uncle Louis was in the little office scrunched up in an old chair, one that still had some padding, a telephone near at hand just in case Dad happened to call with news of a job to bid.

Louis was leaning close to the sputtering little gas-fired space heater warming at least half of his body while three of Werner's men were working at their bench making fittings for downspouts, trying desperately to make the work last until four thirty when we heard the crack of gun shots.

Grinder, a veteran from the First World War knew that sound, one he had heard so many times as he lay in the muddied trenches on French soil many years before. He yelled a warning at Hank and Shorty, then ran to the plate glass window and looked out. Grinder could see through the sleet a commotion, a movement of men on the street in front of Chlem's shop, and Fingers, his back to the street almost onto the sidewalk holding a revolver.

Before Fingers stood Billy, the young apprentice with one withered arm walking toward him calmly holding out his one good hand as if accepting a gift, but as Billy reached for the gun Fingers dropped the weapon to his side, then stared at Billy in a daze.

Before the last shot had sounded, Grinder had raced out the door running toward Fingers with Hank and Shorty close behind. Somehow they knew damned good and well Fingers had done whatever he had intended. As Fingers stood hunched over like an old man, his huge body seemed so much smaller, his head shaking from side to side, the three tinners wrestling him to the wet pavement. While Hank grabbed the gun from Finger's hand, Shorty quivering like an oak leaf in the wind held Fingers down.

Billy was scared. Having seen the shots, he was afraid to look into the shop and yelled to Grinder saying, "Better go inside mister, I think Fingers done kilt Swede."

Sure enough, not thirty feet inside the shop lay Swede, his arms flayed out, blood pouring from his chest. The few men working in Chlem's shop were standing as far away as possible, looking like they might bolt for the rear door, all watching as Grinder knelt over Swede then took one touch of the still figure and shook his head knowing that Swede wasn't gonna screw Fingers' wife ever again.

The entire episode had been missed by Jew Bill, a man with a high regard for his own health and careful to protect it. When the commotion began, he decided in his own type of wisdom to head for Crow's Shoe Shop located three doors down and there to stay hidden. He listened to the crazy Russian, who by now had finished a bottle of moonshine and already was three sheets to the wind, learning more about Communism than he really wanted to know from the shoe maker, cringing at the sounds of gunshots, but laying low until all the ruckus was over.

Jew Bill had sense enough to call Abe when the ruckus started and he arrived in his Cadillac just as an ambulance and two police cars, with four cops to a car and ready for anything since this was Skid Row, came barreling down the street.

There stood Fingers, his head hanging down swaying from side to side, the gun now in Hank's hand as he held one of Fingers' arms while Shorty kept a shaky grasp on the other. All eight of the cops grabbed Fingers at once, roughing him up to show off for Abe. After all, Abe was the guy who owned not one, but two Liquor Stores and passed out free booze at Christmas time.

But there was no fight in Fingers, who stood in a stupor muttering to himself, "Goddamit, I wish I'd shot that damned woman instead of Swede. He was a pretty good guy."

Within an hour the whole thing was over, squashed by Abe whose influence carried far past Skid Row—all the way to City Hall. Fingers was quickly put on trial, convicted of second-degree murder and sent to prison for life in Parchman, a prison in Mississippi noted to be one of the hardest places in the United States to do time.

Within a year, Fingers working with a fellow inmate—both wearing orange jumpsuits and probably in ill humor while chopping cotton in the baking July heat — beat the man to death with his spade before the gunbull riding on horseback some distance away could reach him as he flailed away with his spade at the inmate for simply making fun of his birthmark. Word was that Fingers spent the rest of his days in solitary confinement. It mattered little to him since he had few relatives and the ones he did have didn't give a damn about him.

Swede had been laid to rest in Potter's field, having arrived in Memphis a year before from someplace up North, a town in Maine, someone said. When he was discharged from the Navy, he moved south, ending up in Memphis and calling on Fingers by chance for a job. Fingers put him on, though there was little work for Swede to do. He had no money and very few friends.

When Swede died, the rumor was that Fingers' wife was the only person in attendance and soon after the funeral; she took up with yet another blond ex-sailor, complete with a Scandinavian accent.

When Fingers died, his widow was rumored to have moved to a city up North and dyed her hair a yellowish blonde with a tint of orange, caused by a mix in the selection of dyes applied by a less than sober neighbor. She was also reported to have lost her Southern drawl for a Down East accent no one could understand.

Grinder, Hank, and Shorty all basked in glory for a few weeks until Hank, having stuck Finger's revolver in his back pocket when all the commotion was going on, got drunk at the Red Rose and decided to show all the other drunks how he wrestled the gun from Fingers' grasp and shot the most expensive bottle of whiskey by mistake, getting the three of them banished from the bar for a month, something unheard of at a place with damned few rules of conduct.

Billy became somewhat of a local hero, a kid who had had no illusions about himself and was, from the day of the shooting, so dedicated he became like the son Abe had never had. Up to this point, Billy had been a ragamuffin almost all of his life, no living relatives. When he was just a little kid his Momma had run off, telling Billy's daddy that she couldn't stand to touch, or look at her son's tiny, withered arm ever again. After she ran off, many folks suspected Billy's Uncle to be the scalawag who took up with her, the two of them settling in Tulsa. Billy and his daddy lived a rugged, sad life.

One night when his daddy was drunk talking in tongues, crazy ranting while the two were sitting on the sofa, he suddenly leaned over and kissed Billy on the cheek, said good night as tears ran down his face, left the room and seconds later, Billy heard the blast of a shotgun. When he ran to the bathroom, there in the tub was his daddy, shotgun in hand, head hanging half off his neck. With no place to go, Billy learned to live on the street, sliding down from his old house in south Memphis to Skid Row like so many others had done. A nice kid who had no family, Billy somehow had dodged the booze, never taking to the taste or the way it made him lose control. Soon, he had a decent place to live and Abe had the men help until Billy became a whiz at layout work. Within time, he became one of the best mechanics in the shop.

Billy was a serious person still leading the life of a monk, waking in the morning, going to work then heading back to his little apartment not two blocks from the shop, always refusing in a soft polite voice when asked to go have a few drinks at the Red Rose with the other tinners. Instead, Billy ate at Nick's most nights, even shying away from the young whores on the corner.

When Abe decided to make Billy foreman, he called on my dad, respecting Dad's opinion, knowing he would get the truth from Dad. The two made a strange combination: Dad, a dedicated sheet metal man set in his ways with no give or take and Abe, a jovial, round, bald-headed little guy always with a joke, knowing nothing about the tin business. My dad would say when I asked why he didn't like Abe, "Don't kid yourself JoJo, I ain't got a better friend in the world than Abe Chlem."

When Abe asked about Billy, Dad told him, "I'll tell you what, Abe. If you don't want that kid, I'll take him. He's gonna make a hell of a lot better man than Fingers. The men like him, he's smart, and he's loyal. He ain't gonna walk off from you, even if he gets offered more money."

And so Billy came from a lonely, one-armed street guy, to a shop foreman.

On a spring day when the sun was brightly cutting through the haze and the old buildings seemed to gleam, Billy stood in the doorway of Chlem Sheet Metal just to get a feel of freshness when a girl came out of the Manor across the street and Billy's heart jumped into his throat. Surely that pretty young thing couldn't be one of the high steppers, the very one everyone on the row was talking about.

The word on the street was that she had a baby, a little boy, and that she had moved in with Gertie, and the two older women, but seeing her strolling along, she looked so pure, too young to be in the game and for the first time, Billy felt a queer feeling, a tug in his chest like he never felt before. Billy stood staring across the street when the beauty, Norma Jean by name, looked back right into Billy's eyes, smiled and gave him a wave, not the flirting type, just a friendly gesture, a neighborly type of wave.

Billy waved back in a sly way, not wanting the men in the shop to make fun of him and sure enough, there I was, occasionally referred to by the men as, "That damned little JoJo, the boss's son at Werner's shop," standing in the doorway. Norma Jean leaned over and gave me a peck on the cheek as she passed, then turned again and waved at Billy.

The next day was Saturday and Chlem Sheet Metal was shut tight while Abe went to Synagogue and Billy thought to himself, maybe I'll go over and see if I can find out something about the woman at the Manor.

5

Saturday—A Way To Make Fifty Cents The Hard Way

On Saturday morning I would ride with my dad and Uncle Louis to the new shop—the new shop with the old equipment—Dad pulling up to the curb in the 1938 Plymouth.

Most Saturdays there were small jobs for me, simple projects such as ferrules for hanging gutter or pieces of step flashing for chimneys. At the age of thirteen, I could make a sum of fifty cents for a morning's work but I also had the added benefit of being around men who climbed steeples, worked on hot tar roofs, drank whiskey, cussed up a storm, and chased women.

On those days, the men would drop by the shop; have a few nips and brag about their conquests from the night before. I would have worked for free but my mother would have had a conniption fit if she'd known about it.

My dad, who had been the outside man—the one who ran the work roaming from job to job, seeing that the work was done both properly and on time—had now become the negotiator, replacing Uncle Louis, whose eyesight had failed almost overnight some years before from an unknown affliction. Louis was a special person, a born bullshitter glib of tongue, a good mind, quick with figures, who at one time had been a rounder, drinking with the best of them while closing a deal. He was also one of my best friends.

But now he stood to the side rubbing his sightless eyes as Dad hitched up his belt to hide his overlapping belly, trying not to show how nervous he was, then taking off in the Plymouth to call on general contractors and chum around with guys higher up on the scale, there to out-bullshit the other sheet metal contractors in the hopes of getting a job or two from the few projects that were available. While Dad was gone, Louis would sit by the telephone, batting his blind eyes nervously, his nicotine stained fingers holding the ever present cigarette in the hope that some job, any job, would come their way, one that would keep the doors open for another month.

When Dad returned, usually empty handed, he and Uncle Louis would really get into it, a real shouting match yelling at each other for no reason other than frustration, especially after the mail came with all the past due notices along with damned few checks.

On those Saturday mornings, I was earning my fifty cents working far in the back, where the shop was darkest, trying to avoid the union business agent. With no union card, the contract stipulated that I pick up no more than a broom, a rule that Dad ignored and the union agent overlooked knowing how close the shop was to going under.

Chlem Sheet Metal was closed on Saturday, Abe Chlem probably at Synagogue, and it was somewhat of a ritual for his men along with tinners from other shops to drop by for a nip and possibly hint around for a job, many of the men sitting on the bench like pinch hitters working only two or three days a week. As those Saturdays wore on and summer turned to fall then winter closed in, the number of men increased, the talk turning to a more serious note with some of the half baked tinners becoming formal enough to wear a clean shirt, like it was Sunday-go-to-meeting day.

After a few nips, the easygoing way among the men began to falter and many whose skills were only good enough to be members of a bull gang would begin bragging about their abilities as layout men. At some point when the talk became too heated, Dad could see the possibility of real trouble, maybe even a fight breaking out among the men. He would pipe up saying, "What the hell are you guys fussing about? Hell, we don't have any more work than Abe Chlem, maybe less."

As the morning darkened toward noon, I could hear the congregated men lose hope of getting a free drink and begin talking in muted, serious, even desperate tones about what the weekend held since by now their money was gone, assuming that they had been fortunate enough to have received a brown pay envelope the day before.

Dad, Louis and the regular men could take a little mooching, maybe hand out a small bit of change then run them off like swatting flies. You could see the desperation in their eyes knowing that with Sunday coming the next day, the liquor stores would be closed and plans needed to be made accordingly. Negotiations would soon begin in anticipation of the rest of the weekend. With the only bottle already down to a spider, there was no hope that there would be enough booze to last until Monday. At some point everyone stopped arguing long enough to put their heads together, all knowing that money was the answer. Most of the group had been connected by birth or marriage to a bootlegger and with that, the sad circle would begin.

One guy would proudly pronounce, "I got a quarter," and another would kick in with, "I got fifty cents." The pile of change would gradually accumulate, until there was certainly enough to buy another bottle, one to last the rest of the day and if stretched a little, enough to buy a bottle or two from the bootlegger come Sunday.

Monday would come too soon for this bunch when hopefully someone in the crowd would have a job, maybe even one that lasted a few days. I watched in wonder, staring from the sidelines at those pitiful fools. One of the bums looked as if he might cuff me as I stuck my head in among the crowd but another would jump at him saying, "Hell, leave that boy alone. That's JoJo. He's the boss's son." And I would stay there and stare, even though my head barely reached above the workbench.

I could see my uncle with his sightless eyes blinking, shaking his head in disgust and my dad, who by that time had had a nip or two himself, yelling at the men to get the hell out of his shop. And the remnants of the morning would be gone, the men half tight but desperate for more booze and my dad and uncle worn out, just another day at the shop.

Then there would be the tedious drive home, my dad's voice more of a roar after having a bracer and Uncle Louis, red in the face shaking with fury, cussing the men for being no account but having no answer, sure that their families were at home with a few tins of soup and a potato or two, nothing more. As I listened, pushing myself farther into the back seat wanting to cry but not knowing why, my uncle speaking to Dad but halfway turning toward me would say, "Forget it Joe. There's not a damn thing we can do about it. Hell, we're just barely keeping our heads above water ourselves."

The street people, the ones that would have been on the fringe, were now without the small amount of money that they had mooched from the pile on the bench, spent on wine or canned heat and now left with the bigger problem of a bed for the night. If a drifter has been on Skid Row for any period of time, he had long ago used up all his cash for liquor after having traded in his suit and shoes for used clothing and old tennis shoes.

If the guys had reached bottom, they might have taken a

nosedive, a pledge of religious conviction, which required they listen to a thirty-minute sermon at one of the missions downtown as a last resort. Not only was it against their principles but the odds were the boozers would show up drunk and be tossed out by a converted Christian, one who was usually very large and hated drunks, probably because they reminded him of himself a short time before.

6

One Of Them Things, Part I

As the Depression deepened, the bums and street people still used up their days pacing up and down the street, wandering to nowhere while hoping for a handout, their faces unwashed, lined with sadness and their eyes downcast, chins resting on their chests, searching the ground for a coin that someone may have lost. They would stop at the overhead door and shade their eyes with the palm of a hand then wander on when they saw a shake of the head from one of the men working in the shop.

I was becoming somewhat of a little piss-ant, or so my dad declared two or three times a day. I was fourteen, still scrawny enough to get into the movies on a child's ticket but tough enough for my size, cutting and molding metal all day. If I got lucky I might end up working high in the sky climbing the wooden makeshift scaffold with my old friend Charley to cover steeples with copper. It was one of the few things my dad had reservations about, using me only when he had no one else.

If I left the shop, I was much more likely to be nailing flashing on hot tar roofs. In the shop, I would make sure to work at a bench near a window where I could watch the prostitutes across the weeded lot. In general, I was becoming too big for my britches as my mother often said.

Then an incident happened that changed my life. On a hot summer day, one of those humid suffocating kind that Memphis usually had during July, a guy by the name of Sweeney, known to be a pretty good painter came into the shop through the overhead door. Without slowing as if he were afraid one of the men would stop him, Sweeney went into the little office near the front of the shop where my blind Uncle Louis stood leaning against the jamb batting his nervous, unseeing eyes.

Sweeney hadn't gotten within five feet of the blind man when Uncle Louis turned, his face red with fury saying, "What the hell do you want Sweeney? Go on and get the hell out of my shop before I call the police."

Knowing it was highly unlikely that anyone on Skid Row would call the police and knowing my uncle would be the last one to do so if they did, Sweeney sidled closer to Uncle Louis, causing my uncle to step onto the sidewalk as Sweeney's scent of five cent toilet water wafted through the office.

"Aw, come on Mr. Louis. All I want is a touch till I get paid on Friday."

I watched the tiresome exchange from a bench at the rear of the shop as Uncle Louis continued to raise hell and Sweeney became more desperate in his pleading, Louis knowing that Sweeney had only a part time job and Sweeney knowing that Louis would eventually cave in for fifty cents or so. The whole thing was a farce that was carried on many times a week up and down Skid Row but not by people like Sweeney.

Sweeney stood jittering from one foot to the other, his hopes rising since Louis had not banished him from the office, sure now that my Uncle was good for the bite.

Sweeney was tall and rather thin, muscular in a lanky sort of way with huge hands hanging on arms that reached close to his knees and a bow-legged sort of walk, a poor imitation of a cowboy in a John Wayne western. His hair was tousled and wavy, an old seaman's hat perched on the back of his head just so, and he wore blue coveralls freshly washed with a brilliant pink bandana around his neck formed in the shape of an ascot. Sweeney was one of the bravest guys on Skid Row.

He was what the tinners and street people called, "One of them things."

Along that street and in those times there were no gays or queers, there were just, "Them things."

But Sweeney was also a survivor. He was like a wild man in a fight. He could usually handle more than one punk at a time and if there were too many, he had a sharp jack knife in his back pocket and wasn't afraid to use it.

He and a guy by the name of Otis lived together in the old flophouse around the corner with all the half-hearted construction workers, panhandlers and whores that worked the nearby corner and rented a room by the hour. They occupied a small bedroom no more than twelve feet square situated on the third floor and furnished with a double bed, a small dresser and tiny closet.

The only access to the room was by way of a rickety set of stairs located in the rear of the building making the climb an adventure, especially when one of the stumblebums had dipped too deeply into the bottle. Sweeney and Otis and the other two tenants on that floor made use of the one bathroom at the end of the hall. The two of them had been together since Otis was evicted from his cold water flat above the original Werner sheet metal shop.

In the early years of the Depression, Chlem Sheet Metal Company and Werner Sheet Metal Works had identical shops side by side with only a brick wall separating the two. Above Werner's shop was a cold-water flat occupied by Otis.

When I was a young boy just starting out working at odd jobs, Otis would often scare me to death. He was a squat, bent-kneed little guy with a pointed nose, thick lips, a face fairly covered with warts, ill dressed and smelling of mold and mildew. Otis was a hard worker but was hardly bright enough to work in a bull gang.

I never saw his flat, but heard it was always neat as a pin and dark as the street he lived on with the only light in the flat coming from a cord hung from the ceiling with a single globe attached to a round sheet metal reflector identical to the ones in the sheet metal shop below. Otis's only entrance to his flat was from a tall thin stairway in the alley behind the building. It was attached to a narrow balcony that stuck out from the rear of the building tilting downward from back to front.

Otis would spend his after-work hours relaxing on his veranda, lost in thoughts that only he could fathom, raising his eyes once in a while to stare at the gravel alleyway below, watching the young black children ride their bikes, ones put together with baling wire from remnants of four or five bikes found on a junk pile.

Otis was not a bad guy. I don't think he smoked or drank but he was what my mom would say in a sort of persnickety way, "JoJo, I want you to stay away from Otis, you hear? He's just not our kind."

However, Otis and I soon became a pair, often taking the old pickup with Otis driving and me riding shotgun when we needed metal from a supply house. Once a week the two of us would load up the old scraps and empty liquor bottles then make a run to the city dump. It was a hairy ride, an eerie sound coming from the bed of the truck as the combination of metal and glass met, the two swishing back and forth, making the old 38 Dodge pickup flounder from side to side. It helped none at all that Otis was a less than competent driver but to me it was high adventure.

Still young enough to wear knickers without embarrassment, I never considered that I might be an object for the affection of anyone with the possible exception of my mom and dad. At times on our little jaunts, Otis would give me a fatherly pat on the back or a gentle squeeze of my knee as we drifted along swaying from side to side in the tiny cab of the truck.

Once on a rain soaked afternoon when we had dumped the garbage, scrap metal and whiskey bottles then climbed back into the truck, Otis reached over and hugged me tightly for only a moment but the smell of his clothes and the queasy feeling I got in my stomach made me push away from him as quickly as I could.

No words were spoken but surely even Otis had to feel my resentment. On the ride home from the shop that afternoon, I blurted out to my dad and uncle that I didn't want to go with Otis any more, finally admitting that I didn't like the way he hugged and petted me. There was a grunt and a turn of the head from my dad and a frown as my uncle turned red in the face then an angry look passed between the two of them. There was never a word said. However, within a day Otis was not seen again and when I asked about him, Dad and Uncle Louis ignored me. No one probably including Otis knew that he was gay until Sweeney took up with him and as some of the men said, "Sweeney just turned that boy."

Whatever the reason, the two of them made a most unusual pair. Sweeney always looked nice, well dressed, smart as a whip, a better painter than most, often requested by ladies in expensive homes for special jobs, somehow able to pick colors that fit their tastes while Otis was dense in both body and mind but with a heart filled with goodness.

Since the episode when Otis had put his arm around me, he had been lost until Sweeney came along yet far too often, a feeling of guilt would overwhelm him and life would seem unbearable. Then almost in a trance he would wander down Poplar leaving Skid Row behind until the street reached the Mississippi river with its murky waters lapping at the cobblestones. There he would stand, his round little head with a gimmie hat pulled tight over his forehead staring at that awful current ready to give himself up and walk until the heavy brown waves took his sins away, sins that others had told him he had committed, sins that he felt only a vague guilt about. But now, Otis, the little man with the perpetual smile and pleasing manner was beginning to feel like his old self again, still not completely sure about his role with Sweeney but becoming more comfortable with his feelings as the months passed.

Otis, who had been standing outside of the overhead door while Sweeney had wheedled Louis for a handout, gradually edged into the shop and jumped as if shot when I hollered, "Hi Otis, how you doing?"

When he looked into the darkness and saw that it was me, he recovered his wits and came back to my bench with a sheepish grin.

"JoJo, you scared me half to death back here in the dark."

After stuttering around with his feet for a minute or so, he whispered, "JoJo, do you think your daddy and Louis would put me back on if they got enough work?"

Feeling like somewhat of a negotiator as much as a fourteen-year-old could, I said, "Hell Otis, I'll be glad to talk to them. I never could figure out why they let you go in the first place."

We left it at that but I could feel that Otis was afraid of getting too close, jitterbugging back as we talked. I could feel the tension emulating from Otis and wanted to ease his mind but somehow I was afraid that I might hurt him by speaking up. I had always felt that I was the cause of his firing and wondered how Dad and Uncle Louis didn't realize that every fourteen-year-old in our neighborhood knew what a gay was.

After Sweeney had bummed the fifty cents from Uncle Louis just as I knew he would, and he and Otis made their run to Nick's for a beer, I kept my word and approached my uncle. Louis and my dad were as fond of Otis as I was and with little persuading, they hired Otis once more but with a slight demotion. Now Otis swept the floor and drove the truck but stayed far from me. Whether it was from my dad's instructions, I never knew but in the middle of a Depression, at least it was a job.

7

One Of Them Things, Part II

The flophouse that Sweeney and Otis lived in was two stories tall with a step-pitched gable roof. It was by far the ricketiest building in the entire neighborhood with windows that sat at a awkward angle, most halfway open stuck in place by years of misuse allowing rain or snow to filter in ruining the ceilings, making the old plaster blister and fall in lumps where it stayed until the powdery dust floated away. The paint still visible on the clapboard siding was probably white at one time but through the years had become a dusty grey.

The old building housed a few tinners, some down-and-outers, and of course boozers who barely survived with whatever job they could find to pay the fifty cents it took to keep a roof of some sort over their head. Most were part-time employees of the smaller shops where they worked, usually lasting three or four days before the itch became too much to bear. Their vow to the boss would be forgotten after a really bad night and they would begin showing up late for work then within a week, they would quit showing up at all.

If Dad or Abe needed help badly enough, they would send one of the regulars around the corner where there would be an array of men of all ages and sizes usually sitting rocking chairs or on an old sagging sofa, their heels hooked over the wood railing, a hand rolled cigarette in one hand and a pint of wine or a bottle of beer in the other. But this was the way it had to be since the Union Hall was filled with men sitting on benches there waiting to be called up, knowing that there would be a dash of money to be passed under the table to the shop steward, a common practice but one that infuriated both the honest, hard working tinners and owners like my father and Abe Chlem.

These were the sorriest of times for the small shops, ones who could never promise a full workweek or a decent sized project to work on.

Those were the years when Dad and Louis came closest to giving up, just throwing in the towel. But my dad and uncle were not brought up like that. There was no quit in them. On endless afternoons when winter was coming and it became dark more quickly, I sat in an ugly little office with its old gas space heater spitting and sputtering and watched as Friday stared Dad and Uncle Louis in the eye, which meant another payday to be met. I would watch with sad eyes as they called and badgered, in some cases pleaded, with contractors who were usually in a pinch themselves. And then somehow the money would come in, maybe just enough for one more week, and Dad would cast a fierce look at my uncle and say, "It's okay Brother. We'll just have to tough it out."

With only a few projects on the books, fewer men were working full time. More and more tinners were coming into each shop, ones who would be needed for only a short while, the kind that I hated to be around, the kind of roughnecks who scared me and made Dad a little nervous. When Dad was in a bind—when one of the regulars didn't show up, on a bender or worse—he would send one of his trusted metal workers around the corner to the flophouse where the tinner would gather up two or three of the more stable looking men then put them on ordinary jobs. They were the type of men who knew just the basics about metal work but could do a decent job of installing flashing on a hot tar flat roof, the kind of work that was simple enough but necessary, and they could do it, without killing themselves or someone else.

One of those discards was a guy by the name of Harry Kraft. Surely Carl, the man Dad sent to pluck a guy from the sleepy-eyed bunch wallowing on the porch, could have done a better job of selecting part-time help even from that sorry mess, yet one look at that no-account Harry Kraft and I knew, even at the age of fourteen that there was going to be trouble. Carl was a good mechanic, but he sure as hell was a sorry judge of character. Dad, desperate for help of any kind called Carl aside and said, "You damned fool. What the hell did you bring that trouble maker back for?"

Carl, who was somewhat embarrassed, wasn't very happy himself as he told Dad, "Mister Joe, he was the last one on the porch. One of the whores waiting for a pick-up told me all the others had been run in by the law."

Harry was a surly sort known up and down Skid Row as a bigot and a bully. His clothing was not really dirty but it put off a musty smell, the type of odor that one would associate with clothing that was stored in an attic for a long time. The smell was strong enough to make me turn my head, almost overpowering. Everything about Harry was square—square shoulders with large forearms, square looking hands—and a mop of hair that hung jaggedly over his ears, obviously not familiar with a barber's chair, more than likely hand-cut with a pair of tin snips.

He was taller than the average man, held himself as straight as a re-bar, and had a prissy strut as if trying to prevent the fact that he was knock-kneed. Harry had the meanest eyes I had ever seen with black irises behind bottle-shaped glasses attached to his ears with homemade wire rims. In the weeks to come, I would find him the most evil person that I had ever known.

I had been around the shop long enough to know damned well that I would be stuck with Harry since Dad was sure that all the other men would find an excuse not to work with him. Sure enough Dad called me from the back of the shop where I was trying to hide saying, in a somewhat sheepish tone, "JoJo, you're just gonna need to ride out to Booker T. Washington School with Harry and help finish the base flashing that Grinder started. The damned roofers are about to cover us up."

Grinder was one of the regulars but rarely showed up on Monday, more than likely harboring a terrible hangover from the weekend, something I usually didn't care about but on that day, I hoped his hangover would kill him.

I got in the old Dodge truck after loading a big stack of copper flashing while Harry stood around mouthing off telling dirty jokes to some of the regulars, then rode shotgun while Harry drove, somehow shifting gears and rolling a handmade cigarette at the same time. It was a hotter than normal that day, an edgy feel to it, a day that seemed filled with tension. Even the breeze coming in the window flap was warm enough to make me sweat. I had a queasy feeling in my stomach that wouldn't go away, a sense of trouble down the road, maybe even something serious.

Harry spoke little as he drove only spouting off once in a while about having to work with, "Them damned nigger roofers," as he called them. Slanting his eyes, maybe trying to goose me a little, probably waiting for me to nod in agreement, Harry did not realize that my best friend on that roof was one of the young black roofers.

Once we climbed the ladder and began laying down the copper flashing, Harry surprised me by being a hard worker and a good mechanic but he had a habit of stopping at times then sloping his eyes at one of the black roofers with such hatred his entire body seemed to quiver. His glare was such that the roofer closest to him would inch away surely having seen that look before, knowing that special stare, the kind that felt like a dark cloud on a sunny day, the kind that would bring serious trouble, one that he wanted no part of. The rest of the roofing crew also sensed the glare and tried to ignore it until at last, Harry would shake his head, lean down and begin nailing the flashing to the wood planks as if nothing had happened.

During the following week Grinder showed up each morning sober and on time and things became more normal, except for Harry's strange trances every day. Grinder and I worked closely together, both staying as far from Harry as possible and as he looked at Harry working down the line, Grinder would say, "I ain't never had any use for that son-of-a-bitch. I wish your daddy hadn't hired him."

But, Harry was there and we just had to bear it.

At noon somebody, usually the roofing foreman, would holler, "Eatin' time," and I would climb down the ladder with the rest of the crew and get my paper sack filled with baloney sandwiches, crackers and sweet tea in a jelly jar from the cab of the truck then go sit under an old elm tree.

Most days I was joined by Junior, a tall, skinny kid dressed in thrown-away overalls, the bottoms reaching only to the ankle of his high-topped boots, a plaid cotton shirt with cuffs far too short, probably left to him by an older brother who I suspected had run away and from Junior's account, most likely wanted by the law. Junior and I were much the same while working on a hot roof but far different in many ways. I was a white boy beginning as a freshman at Christian Brothers while Junior was black and had quit school after eighth grade in order to put food on the table for his family.

His Dad was a part of the same sorry story that so many of the roofing crew shared. Beginning at an early age his Dad worked as a helper just as Junior was now doing. Then a mop man wearing the cheapest of sun glasses or old eyeglasses that had been smoked until darkened to help protect his eyesight from the deadly sulfur but failing, Junior's father at the age of forty had lost his eyesight completely. Now it was Junior's turn, the son taking his father's place. There we sat beneath the tree, me and Junior, a young man with little or no hope, no future except the possibility of becoming a foreman, even that damned unlikely since all the foremen were white.

We had been friends since my first day as a helper nailing copper flashing to the wall for a built-up roof. On the morning Junior was handling the pitch bucket, it was so full of the scalding liquid that it sloshed over the sides as he dragged it along on rusty rollers while the roofers mopped the copper flashing to the wood deck. The boiling pitch with its mixture of tar and sulfur could blister our skin in a minute and I noticed that Junior made sure to keep the fumes far from me so that I could attach the copper flashing before the sulfur scalded me.

Junior approached with a troubled look frowning as he asked, "JoJo, what the hell you doing messing with a white man as mean as that son-of-bitch?"

With a shamefaced smile I tried to explain how Dad always put me with the losers.

"Tell ya what Junior, what do you do when your boss puts you with Jackson, the damned fool that mops the pitch? He's meaner than Harry. Hell, he almost swung that pitch bucket in my face this morning."

We stared hard at each other for a minute then like typical fourteen year olds, we started giggling. When we had quieted down, I jumped in with the question that had been bothering me.

"Let me ask you something. Have you ever heard a guy being called, "One of them things?"

There was a long silence, and then Junior burst out laughing. "JoJo, you mean a queer?"

Trying not to grin myself I said, "The crew seems to think because I'm the boss's son and a Catholic to boot, all I know is what the nuns teach me."

With that our conversation drifted on to other subjects, mainly girls, the difference between us like a chasm. Junior was already seeing a girl seriously talking of getting married when he was sixteen or so and starting a family. He loved his mom and dad but felt that they were holding him back. He and his girl had many plans. She was pushing him to finish school, even going at night to someplace that gave free classes. Junior was so far ahead of me it made me dizzy.

Hell, I'd not gotten past first base with a girl and only had kissed one when playing spin the bottle at a party. When I told Junior, instead of laughing he looked wistful and patting me on the back said, "Don't worry JoJo. You got plenty of time to grow up."

When that summer ended we promised that we would stay friends but we both knew that would be never happen. We lived in two different worlds. I never saw Junior after that summer. My fault. Someday I was slated to be a contractor and Junior was still going to be a roofer and while I sat in an office, Junior would sit on a hot roof breathing pitch and sulfur. My only hope was that Junior would sometimes think of me and the way we two kids talked about grown-up things sitting under an old elm tree on that hot Memphis summer. We carried on kidding each other until lunchtime was about over when I asked Junior what had been bothering me.

"What I'm worried about Junior is Harry. He hates queers and with Otis our truck driver being that way, and with him and

Sweeney living in the same place as Harry, I just know there's going to be trouble."

I added, "Harry brags while we're riding home in the truck about all the black whores he fools with, the ones who stand on the corner telling me he doesn't even pay for it and then, when he's had a few drinks, he starts talking about what he's going to do to Otis when he catches him alone. I know that he's been talking to Otis because last week Otis told Dad he might have to quit, but wouldn't tell Dad why."

Junior, who liked Otis about as much as me said, "We can't do anything about it JoJo. I'll say something to Jackson. Maybe he might jump Harry, especially when I tell him Harry's been horning in on those black whores on the corner."

And with that, our half hour was up and we climbed back up the old ladder to put in another four hours of hell.

The weeks grew worse, the heat built each day, and with it the humidity increased until the men hardly spoke. If a roofer bumped a co-worker by chance, even someone they drank with every night, there was likely to be a near fight until someone like Grinder or the roofers' foreman stepped in and gently pushed them apart. Then tempers cooled, the glares faded from their eyes and work resumed.

But Grinder was gone now, that friendly smile, the one to step between two dangerous men and settle things down had worn himself out, done in by the heat, age, and too many nights of drinking. Now it was only Harry and me, just the two of us. I wanted to tell Dad or Uncle Louis that I thought Harry was a crazy man gone over the edge with the heat but I never got the chance.

On a horribly hot afternoon when the sun was burning through the sulfur and our skin too hot to touch, when it was almost quitting time and the tension had become as sharp as a razor, Harry purposely bumped into the mop man and with that all hell broke loose.

The roofers' foreman, a white man by the name of Early jumped off the brick parapet where he had been sitting, slouched back with his felt wide-brimmed hat pulled tight over his forehead, rushed in to get between Harry and the old mop guy, but it was already too late. The old man had casually turned in what seemed like slow motion and used the mop filled with hot pitch to rake across Harry's legs.

Harry screamed with such agony that it scared the fight out of everyone. The hot stuff had soaked his overalls and dripped into his high-topped boots and with one look we could see that Harry was down for a long time. As if the incident had nothing to do with him, the old roofer simply turned and replaced the mop in the bucket as if what he had done was the most natural thing in the world.

Junior jumped in and quickly cut off Harry's pants legs with a hook nosed roofer's knife then pulled off Harry's boots, a sight that made the men turn their heads, the sight of raw flesh so horrible that some turned and gagged. Early, the foreman, grabbed a large jar of Vaseline mixed with some sort of oil, the greasy mess that we used to protect our skin from the pitch fumes and gently began to coat the burns on Harry's legs and feet as he groaned and cursed but gradually quieted down as the ointment at least made the pain bearable.

As Harry was being administered to, the old roofer slowly picked up his hat and gloves, climbed down the wooden ladder, then moved off to the black neighborhood and his rickety house on Lucy Street knowing for sure that he would not have a job the next day, damned lucky if the law didn't show and throw him in jail.

When all was said and done Harry's burns were crippling. The pitch had caused infection and Harry would always walk with a terrible limp. After a few months Harry reappeared but now sitting on the front porch of the old flophouse with the rest of the stumblebums yet not before applying for disability with Dad's insurance company for workman's compensation.

Within a few weeks Dad called me into the little office and there a pleasant young man looking completely out of place, taking quick glances with cautious eyes at the bums wandering by. My blind Uncle was there, standing in the doorway while the man who never stated his name stood in a sopping wet coat and tie, surely dressed for cooler climates than Memphis, asked me right out of the box how old I was and was I the one who had been working on a roof thirty feet in the air around hot pitch. All this was said with one long breath and a concerned expression on his face, as if he were ready to bolt, obviously not used the likes of Skid Row.

Dad saw the way the young man acted, felt the way the wind was blowing and jumped in saying, "Hell Mr. Bowles, this is my son JoJo. All he does is clean up after the men and load the metal onto the truck. He's only fourteen, too young to work on a roof."

Having been briefed, I stood mum as Dad said, "Son, tell Mr. Bowles what you heard happened on the roof that day."

And I lied just as well as I could explaining that the mop man happened to turn as Harry walked by splashing his legs with hot pitch. I didn't add that Harry just got what he deserved and that I was glad to be back in the shop before somebody got killed. Weeks later Werner Sheet Metal received official notice that a Mr. Harry Kraft had been awarded a monthly disability check good for the rest of his lifetime. That should have been the last we would hear of Harry Kraft, but not quite.

Things began getting back to normal, or as close to normal as Skid Row could be. Sweeney and Otis still lived in the old house with the same bunch, including Harry who was now on a cane and wobbled along slowly as he walked, and said little as he sat on the porch pushed back in an old chair, his feet wrapped around the wood railing. However, when the disability money began, Harry quickly took to the bottle and within a few months he could be seen sitting on the old porch drunk or carousing the alley behind the flophouse with an arm around one of the black whores, just kids really from the corner.

Since I was now working in the shop more often than not, I could overhear Carl and a few of the other men discussing the corner whores, their tastes, their costs and their color. The men would have serious debates concerning their weight, their age— most agreeing that the younger girls were not nearly as good a lay, simply laying prone on the old sheetless mattress, legs spread like a bump on a log while the John went about his business—and for a reason that I could never fathom, the size of their rear ends. Those poor souls had been caught up in the Depression. They had no family and no skills except the simple act of laying on their back with some strange man who hopefully would be at least fairly clean and quick and not beat them for being such amateurs at their chosen profession.

These were not the same women as the high-steppers who lived in the apartment next to our shop, who dressed to the nines and traipsed off to Main Street each day. The corner whores were drifters who knew little about the trade but had a willingness to take on a man, almost any man, and worked cheap.

The word was out that Harry had become mean as hell with his women. He stayed drunk and when he got a woman, it was one desperate enough or hungry enough to take him on. Often when he was drunk he couldn't perform and the whore sported a black eye the next day instead of the money she felt she had earned.

As the months passed, Harry talked more and more about Sweeney and Otis always making a slurring remark as the two passed on the way to their room. Otis was so frightened, he came to Dad once and I overheard him say, "Mister Joe, I'm just gonna have to quit. Sweeney and me are going to get our stuff together and head for California. I'm scared that Sweeney's gonna kill Harry if he don't leave me alone."

That same night when the weather had become so cold that the rain was turning to sleet, we lost our poor Otis and what little he had to live for. It was late and the alley behind the flophouse was almost black but for some unknown reason and even though he had been warned, Otis was taking a shortcut home when a pair of strong arms grabbed him and held him tight. Before Otis had a chance to yell, the hand covered his mouth and yanked his pants down then swatted him across the head over and over and back and forth, all the time pushing Otis to his knees.

A voice above him, one he recognized, grabbed him by the ears and said, "Open up Otis, open up."

And with that, the man with Harry's voice raped Otis's mouth while his callused hands held Otis tightly by the ears. As he finished, Harry let out a low moan and staggered, his back hitting the brick wall almost landing on the helpless little Otis as he lay in a puddle on the wet, dirty gravel.

Harry reeled off toward the rear door of the flophouse but not before kicking Otis in the face with his high-topped boots breaking Otis's nose and knocking the little man unconscious. Even then, as if not satisfied, Harry returned once more to kick Otis in the stomach making the little fellow spew the remnants of Harry's seed onto the alley floor.

Otis woke while it was still pitch black to the feel of icy rain dripping from the eave above him stinging his beaten face. His clothes were soaked and filthy wet. He struggled to stand but fell again and again until he got to his feet, his hands bracing against the sooty brick wall. Even after he gained purchase, he fell again, a miserable little man beaten in body and spirit. All the wondrous things that he had felt for the last few months living with Sweeney were gone, now replaced by a shame that could never be forgotten.

With tears running down his broken face, Otis pulled his bruised body together and left the alley behind thinking of only one thing.

Otis staggered down the sidewalk like a drunkard. Falling on the icy street then rising only to fall again, he slowly passed out of Skid Row climbing up the long, sloping hill on Poplar until the street reached a peak then sloped down to where the street finally met the Mississippi.

When he reached the river, Otis searched the ragged ground as he gathered together ice-covered pieces of cobblestone, stuffed his pockets, and then never hesitating, simply pushed himself into the roiling, muddy water until his body disappeared.

There was only one witness, an old man who lived in a cardboard hut near the river but when he described Otis and told the police the following day what he had seen, little was made of the matter. Just another stumble bum from Skid Row who had given himself up to the river, a happening not uncommon, just one less poor fool to watch over.

The loss of Otis affected me for a long time. I missed his smile and I felt guilty for my part in getting Otis fired but it changed others much more. Sweeney became a drunk. A guy who had been so careful about drink took to the bottle and ended up on the street with all the other winos. When his boss fired him, Sweeney became a pest repeating to anyone who would listen that he had turned Otis into something he didn't want to be. On a snowy-cold winter day, Sweeney vanished. A few days later, a stumblebum was seen wandering down the street wearing brown and white oxford shoes, the same type of shoes that Sweeney wore.

When questioned, the bum began hollering, "I didn't steal them old shoes. Hell, they was layin' on the cobble stones down by the river."

But Harry, unlike Sweeney and Otis, didn't choose the way he would leave this old world. He had become an outcast bragging about what he had done to Otis, describing in detail how he had held the little guy by the ears while he raped his mouth until even those bums who sat on the porch of the flophouse and drank Harry's booze, so used to violence, shunned him.

Then late one night, as Harry staggered through the alley behind the flophouse, an arm grabbed him and a razor gave him a gaping red smile as it slit his throat. The Police questioned the corner whores, that being the usual custom, but in the end little more was made of it than the disappearance of Otis or Sweeney.

In the months to come, the bums voiced their own opinions in hushed tones, most remembering that long, sharp flick knife and the one that Sweeney always carried in his hip pocket.

I was a lonely kid after Otis disappeared. The rest of the crew had little time for me. They were too busy trying to make the jobs pay off that my dad had taken too cheaply. I often heard them wonder aloud if he did it intentionally just to have work in the shop, something for the men to do, but also hoping to turn a dollar.

I was just a youngster then, learning a trade, cutting metal flashing all day with a pair of dull snips that often left a trail of blood on the metal where I had cut my hands on the burrs of copper. On those days when I wasn't atop a tile roof or climbing a steeple, my saving grace was Louis, my blind uncle. He and his dear wife Ruth had no children and it was clear that he was as lonely as me but had no inkling how to approach a young man.

With the old radio set on the one station that played country music, the type I hated, Uncle Louis preached to me about women, especially the wrong kind and often asked if I carried rubbers.

He asked me, "For God's sake, do you use them?"

Hell, I thought. I'm only fourteen years old. I never even got to first base, much less in need of a rubber. I loved to listen to Uncle Louis though, so I played along acting more grown-up than I was. He'd soon hit sort of a rhythm and then out would come the stories about when he was a rounder, about the glory days when he was younger before the Depression hit and he had his eyesight. A little smug smile would cross his face and I would grin, hoping that someday I could have memories and stories to tell like that dear man had.

8

Payday

The first time I met Frankie was on a Friday afternoon near quitting time when Dad was doing what he did every week: Sit at his dark green, roll-topped desk and count out the cash for each of the few men working for Werner Sheet Metal Works.

That was the way it was done in the days of the Depression. No checks for those men. They had never seen the inside of a bank but knew what bankers had done to their families, how they had stolen their land, their homes, all their possessions, and most of all, their dignity.

I had just turned sixteen and felt like a grown-up when Dad, too busy to go for himself or so he said, maybe wanting to give me a little responsibility, called me into the office.

"Take this check down to Union Planters and cash it, JoJo and get lots of ones."

Uncle Louis hollered as I went out the door, "And be sure to get some quarters. We never seem to have enough."

I had driven in the '38 Plymouth to the bank and waited there in a long line, a child among adults. Most of the line was made up of contractors. They were men I knew by sight, big men with rough clothes and hoarse voices, too many cigarettes and too much booze, some only halfway kidding with each other to make me fret.

One said, "Hey Jack, you think they'll run out of money before they get to you?"

I was becoming more nervous as the line got shorter until finally reaching the teller, a young looking man not much older than me dressed in an immaculate white shirt with a black snap-on bow tie. He counted the cash from the company check into my hand, which shook like an aspen leaf, then with a smile surely manufactured from his bankers training said, "Have a nice day."

My hands were still shaking as I stashed the money in an old leather moneybag with a zipper on the top and a strap to put around my wrist. I got back in the car and rushed back to the shop afraid of catching hell, the line having been much longer than usual.

When I brought the bag of cash in and laid it down with a dull thump, Dad pulled out the brown pay envelopes from his desk. Then the two of us sat next to each other as he laid out the cash on the scarred surface of the desk, licking his thumb about every third bill as he doled out the dollars, nickels and dimes. I stuffed the envelopes then carefully licked the tab and closed the flap but not before double-checking the amount and adding the proper name in bold letters to the face of the envelope.

The men, all sitting on the work bench closest to the office and passing a bottle of decent whiskey, after all it was Friday, waited their turn to straggle into the little office one after another, grim-faced with a bitterness that showed when they tore the envelope open and slowly counted the meager sum, the bills still wet from Dad's spit. Some of the crew were unable to count without help and on that first day I made the stupid blunder of asking Jesse, a bull gang tinner, "Want me to help you count that money, Jesse?"

Dad gave me a hard look as Jesse's face reddened, then without a word, he turned on his heels and left the office. Those

Friday afternoons my dad and uncle looked like old men, their faces as grim as those of the crew, lines etching their cheeks, feeling for the men, wishing that the envelope could have a lot more bills and a lot less change. It was the one time in the week that transcended the difference between boss and employee.

I sat in the pony chair looking at my dad and uncle seeing mirror images of the tinners. With an almost desperate feeling, I yearned to get up and run and get away from that grown-up way of life but I sat instead, dropping my head, hands gripping the chair, my knuckles white, my eyes burning as they never left the floor.

The tiresome ritual was almost finished when Junior, the truck driver and general clean-up man who had replaced Otis came barreling into the open front door hollering, "Mister Joe, Mister Joe, somebody better come around to the Red Rose. Frankie's over there beating up on Willie and he's gonna kill him if the police don't stop him first."

Dad was pretty sure nobody on Skid Row wanted to have anything to do with the law but since Frankie was to be at the shop bright and early the next morning to make some special copper fittings, he called Hank and Otto, a couple of regulars sitting on a work bench in the back having an after-work nip.

Dad hollered, "Hey, you two. How about running over there and pulling Frankie off Willie? I know Frankie's probably too drunk to hurt the guy but I don't want something to get out of hand."

Hank said, "Hell, Mister Joe. Every time Willie gets drunk he lets his mouth overload his ass. Why don't we just let him be?"

But with a little persuading, Dad, knowing a cop might happen to wander into a place even as rough as the Red Rose, convinced the two to go and they grabbed their coats and trotted out the door with me close behind. I followed them down the block to the dive where most of the tinners met on Friday afternoon to bullshit, sip a few beers and tell lies, before going home. Sure enough, there stood Frankie, calm as could be, his trademark hat still set in place and Willie lying on the floor sort of bloodied up.

When Frankie saw Hank and Otto and realized the fun was over, he reached for the coat rack taking wobbly steps. He pulled on his jacket, adjusted his hat until he was the spitting image of Clark Gable, grinned at the bunch of drunks and staggered out the door.

Everyone agreed that Frankie was the best sheet metal mechanic in the city as long as you could keep him sober. But two things were likely to happen much too often. Frankie would get drunk then disappear for two or three days with a woman, usually his preference of a damned good-looking blonde, or Frankie would get drunk, get in a fight, beat the hell out of some other drunk and end up in jail.

Uncle Louis had known Frankie in the golden days, the days before Louis was blind when Louis himself had been a rounder, the kind of days that still brought a smile and dreamy look to his face as the two of them talked in whispers.

9

Handsome Frankie

Uncle Louis loved to talk and it often happened that he and I were in the shop together, the few men we still were able to employ working on a roof somewhere. On one of those warm spring days, there was the soft murmur of the down-and-outers drifting through the overhead door. The only noise was that of my broom as I swept the metal shavings left by the tinners and the only smell was that of my uncle's endless cigarettes. Louis told me about Frankie's life or as much as he knew about it.

Frankie had come to Memphis from the hills of East Tennessee. He never said but rumor had it that Frankie was putting as many miles as he could between himself and the revenue agents. Everyone, the winos, the thugs, the tinners, hell, even the bimbos agreed that no one would purposely come all the way across the state simply to end up in a city that was broke and on Skid Row in particular, infamous for being the most downtrodden street in a sad, broken southern city on the banks of a muddy river.

Frankie had quickly found his way to a bunch of toughs who just couldn't stay away from the law, often finding themselves in the clinker for minor offences such as being drunk or starting fights with other gangs, the kind of fights that they always won. When the skirmish was over, they would end up in the paddy wagon and the other guys in the hospital. Like most young toughs on Skid Row, there was a rumor that Frankie had been in prison and true or not, it made little difference to the bums that he ran around with.

Frankie had grown up on an eighty-acre plot of scrub brush and stumps, land that was once covered with huge oak trees, now the soil eroding into nothingness. His daddy, who at one time had been a hard-working, church-going farmer planting corn on the forty acres adjacent to the timber, found the tidy sum offered for the trees too tempting, sold the timber off to a lumber company, then like many ignorant men who came into money too easily, turned to the local whores and moonshine. In short order through hard drinking and high living, the old man's money ran out and he turned to the bootlegging business to make a living. It was a known fact that the old man was a prime copper worker, making a still that produced whiskey for all the local dives and juke joints in hills filled with families so poor that a pair of shoes was saved to be worn only on church days.

But somehow there was money enough to change hands for moonshine and as business thrived, Frankie with his two older sisters pitched in to help their daddy, all three beginning at an early age. While Frankie learned copper work and soldering from his daddy, the girls learned to make moonshine, how to keep the temperature just right, and finally, at about the age of fourteen, learned to sight through a clear glass with an inch or so of whiskey to check for sediment and taste the fiery liquid, only a sip, which was swished around in their mouths then swallowed with a huge grin.

Frankie had become an excellent copper worker, a natural warping the metal with a pair of old rollers using copper rivets to attach the joints then applying solder with hot irons and flux, fabricating a still that was more efficient and watertight than anything his daddy would have dreamed. After he coiled the copper pipe into a perfect spiral and set the tap, the end result produced moonshine so pure the bootleggers and honky-tonk owners nearly fought buying as much as his daddy could produce, often paying a premium.

At the age of sixteen Frankie felt like he had the world by the tail. He had grown into a strong, muscular young man able to handle any of the hill boys that constantly challenged him. Those boys, some really big ones, always ended up in the dirt crying more often than not with broken noses at the very least.

Frankie had a quick temper and at times, a meanness when he got out of hand. Once he beat a big old boy, fifty pounds heavier and five years older, half to death and probably would have gone the other half if one of his pals hadn't thrown a five gallon bucket of cold water on his head.

Before long, word spread about the kid with black hair pulled straight back glistening with hair gel and ending in a ducktail. The girls loved it. City girls and country girls alike, they all got wet between their legs when they were with Frankie. Hell, they damned near fought to be with him, lining up to be serviced like heifers by a stud bull. But things were coming to easy and too fast for Frankie. His daddy had given the whole operation over to Frankie, spending all of his time at one of local dives, drinking his own whiskey and laying around with the local whores, none particular, just one who happened to be at hand.

But it was too late for Frankie's momma. She had seen all her husband had done and what Frankie and the two girls had become and one night she simply gave up and went to bed never to rise again, wasting away until she died of a broken heart. As Uncle Louis told it, everything seemed to come to a head at one time.

His sisters, one who had once been a real beauty, had become a roaring, obnoxious drunk. The other sister, just as pretty, found the Savior at a tent meeting being held some five miles away and renounced moonshine as sinful then joined the Preacher, a good looking, well-dressed sort to travel through the hills far and wide never to be seen again. But before she left, the revenue agents began snooping around his daddy's still.

Frankie could see the writing on the wall.

On the first clear night when his older sister was lying on the ground drunk, his daddy gone to a honky-tonk in the woods nearby, and his younger, now-saved sister yelling loud enough to carry all the way up the hill screaming for the Lord to save those poor souls back in the woods, Frankie packed what belongings he had and got the hell out of the East Tennessee hills.

When he sauntered down Skid Row for the first time, he was eighteen, had wide shoulders but not silly wide and was built more like a middleweight. He stood a fraction over six feet tall with jaws set, cheeks protruding as if he had been eating walnuts. His skin was a smooth, silky-cheeked type that fuzz wouldn't show on even if he went an extra day without shaving.

When not at work, Frankie dressed in a suit, granted it was an old suit but shiny as a new penny and it always looked stylish on his tapered figure. He wore a brand new fedora with the suit, brown in color, set at a bias, surely copied off the poster of his idol Clark Gable in the lobby of the Malco Theater on Main Street.

Frankie had a habit of doffing the hat every few minutes, pulling the comb from his rear pocket and running it through his heavily gelled hair. Frankie was the king of the roost, the most handsome man on Skid Row.

10

Frankie And Reba Get Hitched

Frankie pulled into the washed gravel driveway, yanked on the hand brake as he slid to a stop and let the headlights shine on a hand painted sign with the inscription, "James Black, Justice of the Peace," suspended by wire from the eave of the little house.

The cottage sat some hundred yards off the highway, a few miles south of Memphis over the state line into Mississippi where, unlike Tennessee, a couple could get married without the usual waiting period of three days.

Reba sat next to Frankie togged out in a tight fitting red dress, one of the latest fashions, a top-of-the-line piece that she wore when modeling at Bry's Department Store. With it she wore shiny black leather shoes with the highest heels available to both show off her shapely legs and make her seem taller than her slender five-feet-two-inch frame. Of course the dress wasn't hers nor were the shoes; she had simply put them in an old shopping bag as she left the dressing room, sort of borrowing them for the occasion. She had no intention of stealing the items; instead, thinking of them as being on loan to her until the next day.

Reba watched Frankie from across the seat, her head lying against the open window, long, black hair flying in the wind, her legs crunched under her tiny bottom staring frankly at his handsome profile, he in his double-breasted brown suit and bright green tie topped by the ever present felt hat set at a rakish angle, the one that he copied off the Clark Gable poster.

Reba's head was swimming a little from the booze but mostly in wonder. What the hell am I getting myself into, she thought.

"I'm about to marry a guy who is just as likely to get drunk, run off for days laying up with some woman, probably never have any money and a damned tinner to boot," she said to a friend, just hours before.

But Reba knew she was smart, smart enough for both of them. Hell, she had even taken business classes at St. Thomas and always received straight A's. The way she figured it, with her brains and Frankie's way with people, they would make a go of it.

Reba dreamed on saying to her friend, "Hell, this damned Depression can't last forever and when it picks up, Frankie and me are gonna get our own sheet metal shop."

Frankie and Reba had been courting for a while. Frankie had shown her tenderness in his manners, no bragging and no rough stuff. As a normal matter, he expected her to go to bed with him the first time they went out but Reba turned him down in a gentle but firm way. He took the no without a fuss, maybe a little too easy, maybe because he had someone waiting around the corner, just in case she said no, she thought to herself. When Reba slid between the sheets on the second go-round, she found Frankie to be a gentle, comfortable, maddeningly slow lover. Reba lay in his arms, glued to Frankie by their common sweat and thought this guy is nothing like what she expected, sure as hell not like those few times in high school where it always happened in a back seat, the other kid far too anxious, just wham-bam, thank you ma'am.

Frankie was different. He was not the best at using proper grammar and quick with his temper but he had a knack at handling people, a slow, easy, manner that instilled confidence in him even with the bosses he worked for. Yes, indeed, Frankie was a born salesman, if ever there was one.

The two had decided to get married just hours before, after having a few drinks at Nick's, Frankie maybe having gotten a head start by having an extra few before meeting up with Reba. He was pushing past the point of being tight, that period when a man was floating, sort of in limbo, not drunk but a hell of a long way from being sober.

Now Reba sat as Frankie cruised them down the highway in a borrowed Ford convertible with Lester, an old crony and good old boy who owned the car passed out on the back seat, having been promised by Frankie that he could be best man. Reba had no objections to Lester, hell this was a honey of a car but she wondered if she and Frankie would be able to get him sober enough to even stand up when they got there.

Reba first saw Frankie when she and a few of her friends from Bry's Department Store were slumming, all four living in a boarding house on Court Street only a few blocks from Skid Row. The four all had jobs as sales clerks at the most exclusive department store in Memphis and Reba often filled in as a model when the newer fashions arrived. She and her friends, all citified girls, decided to be adventurous one evening when May dared the rest of the foursome to go to a local dive smack in the middle of Skid Row.

Nick's Café wasn't really a dive. It was more like a beer joint but it was a Friday night and the tinners from the area, at least the ones who still had jobs, had been paid and before heading for the Red Rose where most of the tough girls hung out, they went looking to wet their whistles and knock back a few, starting with a shot of whisky and a glass of beer at Nick's.

When the girls came through the door, three dressed in cheap cotton dresses and Reba clad in the fanciest dress the store carried, the place became as quiet as a funeral parlor. This bunch of girls were sure as hell not from the house next door where the high-steppers lived, the ones who came in once in a while to have a drink and test the waters before going to a high-class joint downtown.

Frankie, who was the only one in the bunch dressed in a coat and tie and already three sheets to the wind, turned from the sudden silence and saw three rather chubby girls and one standing slightly aside, a little over five feet tall in three inch heels and with a figure men prayed for.

The three girls all in their early twenties looked shocked, all three turning pale, ready to bolt before they were five feet into the place but Reba took one look at that handsome devil slouched at the table in the rear with his half drunk buddies surrounding him and knew that she wasn't going anywhere. She liked what she saw and intended to push a little just to see where it would lead.

One of the skittish girls grabbed Reba's hand, saying, "Let's get the hell of here before we all get raped."

But Reba pushed her friend away, strutted to the back table swinging her hips.

She stuck out her hand and said to Frankie, "Hi, my name's Reba, what's yours?"

11

Reba's Story

Reba had grown up in a rough area of South Memphis on Guthry, an alley-like street, living in a shotgun house identical to all the others on the block. The street was full of potholes, the curbs were busted, and dirt swirled in the grassless yards.

During the summer, the tables and floors were covered with dust drifting through the open windows. The shoeless children left footprints on the bare wooden floors and their beds stayed grey from the grit, which drifted in from the patched-up screens. It was a typical neighborhood during the Depression, full of men who had given up and women who were trying to hold the family together. Her momma used to say that every man on the street was a drinking man including her daddy right up until the time he was killed.

Reba's momma's name was Annie, a pure Irish lass, pretty as a picture with a voice that came straight from Galway, a devout Catholic and strong in her devotion, a woman who went to mass every day and was determined that Reba would attend St. Thomas School and be raised with a Catholic education. It was an unbearable situation since they lived in a house owned by her mother-in-law and next-door neighbor, a saved again, five-times-a-week, church-going Pentecostal.

Reba's Daddy hardly entered into her life as she grew up. She couldn't remember much about him but somehow knew he was a weak man and would later think of him as a momma's boy. As a child she would sit at her window and watch as her daddy sat at the kitchen table in his mother's house next door, most likely pleading for money and instead getting a finger-shaking tirade and a quote from the scriptures as his mother ranted at the fool for marrying not only a Catholic but an Irish Catholic.

When her Daddy returned from one of those visits, Reba would close her door, squirm into her little closet and hum trying to shut out the racket while her momma would stand stiff as a board as her daddy searched into all his hidey holes until he found a piece of a pint of moonshine. His face would turn crimson as he downed the liquor and soon there would be the sound of breaking chairs and glass then the yelling, her momma giving as good as she got until her daddy left staggering down the street trying to find a buddy, one that had a free drink.

Reba's life changed when she was in the eighth grade.

Her daddy was a railroad man working in the rail yard repairing the old coal-fired engines making them last for just one last trip to Knoxville and back. It was hard, dirty work and her daddy would come home covered with greasy dirt, heels dragging. But it was a job and it put food on the table, even if it was chicken necks and collard greens. Then the Depression deepened.

The engines pulling out of the rail yard now had less cars and one day her daddy came home and told his momma that the bosses had cut wages and the union men were threatening to strike. Within a month, negotiations broke down between bosses and the union. The men went on strike then threw up a picket line at the entrance to the rail yard. Surely in a ploy that was preplanned, the company brought in scabs and with them, troops from an Army cavalry unit stationed on the banks of the

Mississippi, one that had arrived only a week before.

The scabs for the most part were older men from other parts of the county, simply worn-down fellows with families half-starved at home who went about their work in a halfhearted way, hating the idea of taking another man's job but unwilling to let their own families starve.

The soldiers on horseback were a different story, for the most part. They were just overgrown kids bored to death from doing nothing but cleaning out horseshit from the stables. On the day the trains were to leave, the soldiers charged the strikers swinging their batons, yelling like banshees. The scabs followed behind the train as it pulled slowly out of the yard as the strikers threw firecrackers at the horses and rocks at the engineers.

Reba's daddy was a strict union man who hated scabs and loved a fight. As the cavalry closed in, he and a few others stood their ground. When one of the soldiers swung a rifle butt, Reba's daddy grabbed the stock and threw the man to the ground. As he looked down he saw a kid probably no older than his seventeen-year-old nephew and stepped back, feeling only shame. At that instant there was a rifle shot and Reba' daddy folded, killed by a bullet from the gun of a kid no older than the one on the ground.

The killing marked the end of the strike. Somehow the scabs disappeared, the cavalry was gone, and Reba's daddy became somewhat of a folk hero, spoken about honorably in the tavern as the railroad men drank their pints at the local pub. But the union never got its raise, forcing Reba's momma to clean houses to make ends meet and Reba to quit school and go to work at Bry's Department Store as a sales clerk.

12

Frankie And Reba Get Hitched, Part II

Frankie opened the door and half stumbled out of the car all of a sudden feeling sober, maybe a little bit scared. He and Reba had a thing going but he thought to himself that these are some awful rough waters he was heading into.

He mumbled aloud, "I ain't too sure I'm ready for this home life stuff."

Then Frankie looked back at that pretty little thing showing her cute behind as she slid out of the convertible and he shook his head adding, "Oh, shit. Why not?"

Between the two of them, Frankie and Reba pulled Lester out of the back seat and while Frankie shook him like a rag doll, Reba straightened his tie. From the color, she thought his tie must have been the booby prize at a party, then the three of them barged through the door as an astonished preacher, who had been waiting after their call saying they were on their way, slowly stood up from the chair where he had been quietly taking a doze, now shaking his head.

The preacher mumbled, "I married some wild looking ones in my life, but this beats all get out."

Then he called to the room behind him, "Hon, we got a

couple to marry out here. I'll need you as a witness," he said, all the while hoping the one in the middle, the one with the Christmas tie on, the one the other two were holding up, was not the groom.

The ceremony was quick, the preacher tying the knot but not before the twosome got Lester straightened up, though he leaned against the wall during the entire ceremony and looked as if he might slide down it any minute.

Before beginning, the preacher had turned to Frankie and asked the big old boy, "You gonna take that there hat off during the ceremony?"

With that, the preacher said the words so fast that Frankie and Reba understood only the Amen part and then certificate in hand, they were as one, just like the preacher said.

As the convertible pulled out of the gravel driveway spewing rocks in all directions, the preacher said, "Lord, please let them folks get home without killin' themselves or somebody else."

I knew something was up a couple of days later when I walked into Dad's tiny office and it was overloaded with people. There was my dad, Uncle Louis, Abe Chlem, Frankie and Reba.

Frankie saw me and gave me that shit-eating grin then Dad turned saying, "JoJo, get the hell out of here and go back in the shop. Can't you see we're talking business?"

I started to say, Well hell, I'm in high school now and I'm part of the business, but I just shrugged, then backed out knowing damned well that I was going to listen at the closed door.

And what I heard was Abe saying, "Well, if you two are damned fool enough to start a shop in the middle of the Depression, then I'll throw what little extra work I've got your way."

I could hear Dad grumble and Uncle Louis snicker but hell; they always did that just to show how tough they were.

Then Uncle Louis, always the first to give in considering himself a hell of a lot more of a gentleman than my dad said, "May

God help you 'cause you're gonna need it but we're like Abe. We're all in the same boat, so sure we'll help."

And that's how I found out that there was a new sheet metal shop in town.

13

Reba And Frankie Scrape Out A Living

Reba stood on the icy gravel in men's high-topped boots wearing a ratty old coat as she hefted the bucket of hot water and poured it across the windshield.

The thin coat of ice melted onto the hood of the pickup as Reba muttered to herself, "When the hell are we gonna get a better truck? This damned thing ain't gonna last another year."

Reba continued to mutter until finally, she had the windshield cleared, the sputtering engine started, the cab warming, and was ready for another run to the job where Frankie waited.

It had been a year since Reba had convinced Frankie to quit Wall Sheet Metal and start his own business by talking to the Werners and Abe Chlem, convincing them to throw a little scrap of work their way. Reba knew that she was smart with figures and Frankie was a damned hard worker and a good mechanic, even with the ever-present hangover. She had saved a little money and had a good friend in Mr. Stevens, one of the big shots at Bry's Department Store. In fact, he had loaned her the hefty sum of $1,000.

Reba used her cute little body as collateral, often playing up to him as she strutted down the runway modeling the latest fashions, giving an extra lift to the hem as she pranced before him.

She never said that Mr. Stevens was going to get what he surely had in mind, but being a natural born tease, she left a number of not very subtle hints.

However, Mr. Stevens had not become a big shot by being a fool.

He liked Reba and endured Frankie and could see that there was a chance of them making money, maybe not much, but the two percent interest that he charged Reba was far better than the bank paid. And Stevens would, by God, see to it that those monthly installments were met.

Reba was just finishing the windshield when Do-Right and Clovis walked into the yard, both looking like death warmed over. Neither was dressed for the cold weather, not even a heavy coat between them and both looked as if they had slept in their overalls, light shirts, sockless, with tongues lolling out of their unlaced boots.

Clovis, the less jittery of the two spoke up with a smile that showed off a couple of missing teeth.

"Well, Miss Reba, you think that ole truck is gonna make it out to Cordova? I imagine Frankie's needin' some help about now," he said.

Reba never even looked at the two sorry excuses for tinners. Even with her back to them, she could smell the rancid odor of the booze from the night before.

"Both of you get in the back. I ain't gonna let you ride in the cab, not the way you smell," she said.

She hopped up in the truck while the two shiftless bums, afraid to argue with her having a taste of that tongue before, fought to get a hold on the truck bed and climbed in, both shaking so badly that the truck moved back and forth like a swing in a soft breeze.

Once Reba started down Poplar where the streets were clear, she felt a little better, the heater going full blast, warming the cab even more, but not nearly enough, what with two big holes in the floor, one on each side of the axle hump. She could clearly see the pavement fly by and pulled her feet away from the water that splashed onto the floorboard from rain the previous evening. Adding to the misery was the window, the one on the driver's side, which would only halfway close, the glass tilting from back to front as they rode over the rough streets.

She had given thought that the two men might be more comfortable in the front but, remembering that rancid smell, decided the fresh air might aid their hangover. Reba was remembering the little free time that she and Frankie had after they were married. They had not even had time for a real honeymoon, just one night in an upper-class motel, one of the ones far out on Lamar way past the hot-bed types. After a meal and a few drinks at an eight-stool diner attached to the motel and just a short distance from their room, Frankie and Reba retired to the room complete with oil paintings, two of snow capped mountains and one of an ice covered stream, the sort of paintings that Reba had seen many times before, probably bought at some flea market.

There was a small dresser in one corner, one with only three drawers, a small mirror and a large double bed with a machine attached to the side with a quarter slot. Frankie showed her how the bed would jiggle up a storm for five minutes just as they were having sex and Frankie had a pocketful of quarters. Boy, she thought. That sure was fun. Maybe, Reba thought, we can buy one of those gadgets after we make some money.

Reba was getting her mind away from the present, so much so, that she almost ran a red light, had to slam on the brakes, and heard two hard thumps but hearing the yelling, figured at the most, those ole boys were just getting sobered up a little.

Frankie had casually mentioned that morning just as one of Chlem's men dropped by to pick him up, that there was a job right down the road that Do-Right and Clovis might need to stop at on the way out but Frankie instructed, "Only for a minute, Honey."

Reba knew that anytime Frankie used that term he had something up his sleeve and sure enough there seemed to be a banging noise coming from the back. When she looked out the clouded rear window, Reba could see Clovis waving his arms and Do-Right banging on the cab of the truck.

As she pulled to the side of the road, Clovis leaned into the half open window yelling, "Miss Reba, you need to pull onto that gravel lot over yonder for just a minute. Me and Do-Right got some business to take care of."

One glance at that old shack with a tar papered roof and artificial brick siding sitting on a gravel lot half covered with weeds under a concrete bridge to boot and Reba knew exactly what Frankie knew.

With that Reba pulled back onto the road hollering back to the two desperate tinners, "I knew that was a bootlegger back yonder but you two boys are gonna work sober today."

At first there was banging and cussing but then the rest of the way out Poplar to the job in Cordova, there was a kind of a sad silence. As the truck slid onto the job site, Frankie stood, hands on hips grinning like a Cheshire cat until he saw the men frowning, shaking their heads in unison.

Then turned on Reba, saying, "I thought you was gonna stop for those two boys, Honey. What the hell's the matter with you?"

Reba still in men's high top boots, her dress wet as hell and chilled to the bone yelled back, "I knew something was wrong when I got that honey crap this morning. Well, you and them boys both are gonna work sober today 'cause I'm leaving with the truck."

Reba had a worrisome drive back to the shop not even giving Frankie a goodbye kiss; just jumping in the pick-up after the men unloaded the material.

"Damn, I hope Frankie ain't gonna turn into one of them bums and start drinking all day. I know he gets a nip before he leaves the house and that don't bother me none but I don't want him crawlin' into the bottle the way my daddy did," Reba mumbled aloud on the drive back to the shop.

Reba remembered how drink had been part of her life since she was a child just as it had been part of the hopelessness of the Depression. It was the only way men forgot. It had become part of their make-up. She recalled how families often did without food and clothing because the man of the house was out drinking up his wages on a Friday afternoon. Then as times worsened, she remembered as the man of the house would bring home a bottle, pull out two jelly jars from the shelf over a sink with rust colored streaks running down the sides then sit at the kitchen table where often his wife would plop down and dig in putting away the moonshine right along with him until the bottle was empty. That was typical of Reba's daddy and her momma. Most always, if there weren't a fuss with cussing and glass throwing, the two would hold each other and cry, sharing their desperation in a drunken stupor.

Then Reba, thinking of this began to cry, even as tough as she was, saying aloud to no one but herself, "This ain't gonna happen to us. We're gonna tough this damned Depression out."

Reba parked the old truck in the wet gravel lot and turned looking up at the unpainted building, one that Abe owned and had rented to them on the cheap, one of the many small investments that he had scattered throughout the city.

The building was located directly behind the flophouse and had the appearance of an addition to a much larger building, sort of squashed inward yet bulging out like a big toe. The first floor was wide open, plenty big enough for a decent-sized shop but with few windows, not enough light globes and permeated with a dark, dank smell. Their shop had almost no equipment but it mattered little since most all of the work was tile and slate roofing, the two things that required almost no machines or material, only strong backs and a certain amount of know-how.

Soon Reba was determined to have enough money for new equipment and more copper for the type of fancy metalwork that Frankie was good at, but for now they scrapped by repairing the big homes in the high-class areas around Memphis like Central Gardens and Hein Park.

No one was in the shop although Black Robert was to have been at the door bright and early making fittings for Frankie. Black Robert must be hung over again she thought, so Reba climbed the steps to their apartment, which covered the entire floor above the shop.

As usual, she counted the steps, all forty of them to the kitchen which served as an office. There was little use for a desk. The table that did double duty for both eating and office work still had room enough for a telephone and note pad. She made a few calls to the big shots who owned those homes using her politest voice with a little throaty, sexy sound to it and collected enough to make payroll for the next week in addition to a partial payment on the bill owed to Delta Sheet Metal Supply Co.

She knew that before long it would be necessary to call on Mr. Lewis, the old son-of-a-bitch who had owed them a healthy sum for work done on his house, a large part of it overdue by three months. When Reba brought Mr. Lewis's name up, Frankie blew up.

"Reba, that old man's trying to get in your pants. You just let me handle it. I'll go over there and beat it out of him," Frankie said.

But Reba knew that if Frankie pulled a stunt like that, it would be the end since Mr. Lewis, horny old son-of-a-bitch or not, was by far the biggest client that they had.

"Just let me handle it Frankie," Reba had told him.

After checking to be sure Black Robert wasn't going to show, Reba kicked off the old men's work boots and wet dress, changed into a high fashion dress from Bry's, one that had fallen out of the back of a truck, made up her face, heavy with the lipstick, and slipped into her highest heels, the ones with the strapless backs.

Reba got into the pick-up, was thankful that the wind had died, drove to a large building on Union, which Mr. Lewis owned, and hiding the old truck around the corner, she sashayed into the office where she walked past the receptionist giving her a wink and getting one in return as she marched into the old man's office.

Reba was ready to put on her act as he came into the room, the one she used with people like Mr. Lewis but before she could say a word, a very large, older woman, one who was leaning halfway across the desk turned and stared at Reba with a bright crimson face, saying, "You old bastard! Who is this, another one of your whores?"

"Now Emily, stop that nonsense," said Mr. Lewis, shading his eyes, as if in shame. "This young lady is only here to collect for work we're having work done on one of the houses you own."

Then without a glance, he began writing a check for the full amount though Reba had intended to ask only for a partial payment, sitting quietly during the entire transaction as Mrs. Lewis was giving her the evil eye the entire time.

Reba left with check in hand and headed to Delta Supply where she made a decent payment and in return, Woodrow, the owner's son loaded two bundles of copper, plenty for the work that they had on the books. That night, for the first time in months, Reba and Frankie felt relief, even if it was short lived. They knew that Chlem and Werner were both having a tough time of it, even laying off some of their good men and the extra work that been coming to them from the Clem and Werner shops had dried up.

It was a Friday night, the one evening each week Reba

allowed herself to let her hair down when she and Frankie sat in Lester's convertible, cruised around town, ate a good meal in one of the better joints, got a little tight, then went back to their little apartment and made love for hours.

Frankie always had too much to drink, but it never stopped him from being a tireless lover so that afterward, Reba would curl up under the covers and get a good night's sleep with a smile on her face.

14

The Hail Storm

On a Saturday afternoon in April, just about a month or two into the time Frankie and Reba had went off and started their business, my pals and I went to the movie. It was a matinee, and a double feature to boot, and, as usual I got in on a child's ticket. Even though I was fourteen, I was small and skinny. The teller, a kid not much older than me smiled; after all, it wasn't his money.

It was a comforting habit, sitting with my buddies in the dark, paying little attention to the movie, staring at the giggling girls scattered in seats directly in front of us, kicking the back of their seats, just to let them know that we were there, instead of being one of the rough talking tinners that I worked with all week.

As the second feature started, the three of us paying more attention to the silly girls than the movie, there was a frightening clash, the theater lights flickered, then died, followed by a banging noise, which quickly became a rumble.

Without thinking, my two friends jumped from their seats with me close behind, girls forgotten, as the three of us ran for an exit. Thinking the building was ready to collapse, we flew past the milling mob in the lobby and ran onto the sidewalk where we stopped and stood in wonder, staring at hail stones that covered the ground, not the ordinary type, but hail stones as big as baseballs.

Following on Sunday morning, the day after the hailstorm, I was scrunched down in the back seat of Dad's car, still half asleep. Dad was driving the old Plymouth, heading for the shop as Louis sat in front, arm out the window, wind flap turned out trying to catch a little breeze.

Louis opened up with, "It's a damn good thing that hailstorm hit us, Joe. I don't think we could have lasted another winter."

Sitting there I thought to myself, thanks to the hailstorm we'll make it. Abe Chlem will make it and maybe even Frankie and Reba will make it. But Dad never wanting to admit such a thing said, with a wry grin my blind Uncle couldn't see, "Ah shit Louis, we been through this before. We could've just toughed it out like last winter."

Even a fourteen-year-old kid like me knew this wasn't true and as he spoke, he looked at me in the rear view mirror with an expression that told me that Uncle Louis was probably right. Business had reached a terrible low, so much so that every one of Werner's crew were working part time, some so desperate that they sidled up to Louis when no one was around whispering in his ear, offering to work for less than the union wage.

The union business agent, a retired sheet metal worker himself and a good, fair man often came around the shop talking to the men trying to encourage them saying, "It'll get better men. Hell, we've gone through this kind of thing before."

Then he talked to Dad asking if there were any jobs that he could help in securing, some work maybe through the new programs that the government had instigated. Dad and Louis who usually hollered at each other at any time that they were within speaking distance were now quiet, speaking in low tones, heads close together, wanting no one to overhear mostly about the bills that kept piling up and how they were going to hopefully collect enough money to pay them and whether or not they were going to have enough in the bank to make the weekly payroll or if they might have to lay a man off and if so, which one.

Within the last few months Dad began taking on little jobs, ones with contractors who had a bad name, unlikely to pay their bills within three months if at all, then Uncle Louis, always good on the telephone, would use his magic and somehow, within a few days the guy would show up at the door with a check. Knowing it was going to bounce, Dad, onto that scheme, would demand cash. After a little negotiating, the contractor would leave with a smile and Dad and Louis, a beaten look on their faces, had the green in their hands on a job that made no money but gave the men a few days work.

The tinners who worked for Werner were no fools. They knew those fly-by-nights by name and reputation and they knew that Dad had taken a chance even doing business with such shady characters. It made for an unspoken kinship; the tinners putting everything they had into the job knowing it was sink or swim, for bosses and men alike.

Then came that Saturday afternoon when the hail stones thundered through a large part of Memphis destroying tile and slate roofs along with cars, windows, and skylights and the telephone in our home, the one sitting in the hallway began ringing off the wall.

Insurance companies who had written policies for Werner Sheet Metal, probably sorry to have done so knowing they were going to need months to collect the premiums and then probably receive only partial payments, were the first to call. The agent, sometimes even the owner of the insurance company was calling needing men to repair the roofs so damaged that they were open to the elements reminding Dad of the way that they had carried Werner Sheet Metal over the years.

Dad may not have been much of a businessman but he was

tough as a dime steak when he needed to be, yet he was always a fair man, a man of his word and he readily agreed with those gentlemen, assuring them that their clients would be first to get their roofs repaired.

Then came strangers, insurance adjusters, and the guys in suits and ties, ones who worked for some home office Dad had never heard of. They were calling, some even coming to our front door. They were the kind who wouldn't give Dad the time of day just a month before and now they were calling, some pleading, others badgering, wanting to be first in line to get tile and slate roofs repaired, many even replaced.

The hail had hit hard but passed within minutes. Dad trying to be sympathetic said with a halfway guilty grin, "Half of the tile and slate roofs in town are busted to pieces."

Dad called Louis and the two of them began contacting the men trying to round up a crew, even a half assed one for the next day, knowing it was damned unlikely that he could find one, and if he did, one that would be sober.

Things were quickly getting out of hand. Charley, the only one of the men who didn't drink, promised to work even though it was Sunday but only after going to church. He also told Dad, "Joe, I talked to Hank and Cal and they promised to be at the shop tomorrow morning but the way they're laying out on Cal's front porch, it ain't likely that they'll be sober by tomorrow."

When Dad came into the living room he took one look at me and said, "JoJo, you're just gonna have to work tomorrow with Charley. I can't seem to find nobody else," and when he finished saying those few words, I thought Mom was going to have a fit. Mom wasn't strict about many things; in fact, she let us get by with more than most mothers in our neighborhood, but Mass was a must on every Sunday, especially since I was an altar boy. When she put her foot down, of course Dad lost but only halfway saying, "All right, but JoJo, after mass you're gonna pull up tile for Charley, and I'll get a boy to help you. Then you can take off from school for the next couple of weeks."

Sunday mornings had a strange sort of quietness on Skid Row. The down-and-outers were laying out somewhere passed out or sleeping one off. The Manor next door was quiet as a tomb, the high steppers not ready to stir for another few hours. Hell, even Nick's Café and Crow's Shoe Shop were locked up.

Dad pulled the Plymouth into the curb telling Louis, "Charley sure does look lonesome standing there by himself. There ain't another soul around. I reckon we'll just make do with him and JoJo for today."

I piled out of the car all the while thinking about standing on the ground all day at some huge home on a tree-lined street pulling up tile on a rope with a block and tackle while Charley repaired somebody's roof, him moving like a cat the same way he did when he scaled a steeple. Just the thought was beginning to give me a stomachache.

Time was wasting. The telephone was already ringing; Louis telling people that things were getting cranked up and just to hold their horses, a statement that both he and the client knew was a damned lie. The best thing going for Dad and Louis was the tile and slate stashed in the back yard. Everyone knew that Werner Sheet Metal had always done the bulk of roofing in Memphis and over the years, the tile and slate had accumulated until they filled a large shed. Dad had complained for years that we should just take them to the dump, but somehow the pile never moved. It just kept growing, getting higher and higher.

Now he felt like he had fallen into an outhouse and come out smelling like a rose. That accumulation of tile and slate was going to be the answer to Werner's prayer but Charley and JoJo couldn't touch the amount of work that was sitting out there. Dad and Louis knew that other shops were gearing up with enough work for a few months as soon as they had the material, but for now Werner was king of the hill. As long as they could get the work done.

As Louis called roofers, guys who knew tile and slate work, Dad went around the corner to the flophouse trying to scrape up extra help while Charley and I began loading up the pick-up with tile, the type needed for the first job, a house located in an upscale neighborhood named Central Gardens and owned by the president of our local bank.

About the time we had the tile pushing the truck springs down to the breaking point, Charley called a halt and we sat waiting for a ride to the job. A yellow convertible came roaring down Poplar. In the front seat sat Frankie and driving was Lester, Frankie's gambling friend, the one with the ugly tie and best man at his wedding, the same Lester who kept sliding down the wall while the Justice of the Peace stood with jaw opened in wonder.

In the back seat was Ewell, Frankie's all round man, a do everything sort of fellow. Ewell was Reba's cousin and only living relative. Part time tinner, truck driver, roofer and general gofer, Ewell also lived with Frankie and Reba and although Frankie liked him, Ewell was a thorn in Frankie's side being that the little apartment would hardly fit the two of them, much less a six foot something farm boy who didn't drink or smoke and far as Frankie could tell, didn't screw.

Frankie jumped out waving as Dad was returning from the flophouse shaking his head in disgust, having found nothing but a couple of bums sitting on the porch with a bottle of beer.

Frankie said, "Hey Joe. I been trying to call your house. I wanted to see you about some of them tile and slate you got in your back yard. I come by thinking maybe we can make a deal."

Frankie said everything at once then looked around kind of

embarrassed, being that he was a little the worse for wear, listing a little as he leaned on the trunk of the car but his hat still set firmly in place at that rakish angle.

Dad knew that Frankie was a crackerjack at roofing and also knew that he and Reba were having a tough time of it. He glanced at Louis and got a little nod of the blind man's head then must have come to a decision right then and there. Dad waved him into the office. Frankie plopped down into the chair that I was going to claim after Dad ran me out into the shop, something that I was getting tired of while they made a deal.

Dad stood over Frankie seeming to give it some thought then looked at Louis and said, "What we'll do is this Frankie. There's a plenty of business for everybody if we handle this right."

And Dad added, "Now, we've got most of the tile and slate that might be needed, but we got to move fast. Those other outfits can order the material and have it here in four to six weeks, but in the meantime, we can make a killing."

Then Louis piped up, "Where are we going to get the men, Joe?"

And Frankie gave him that slick look he saved for special occasions saying, "You let me worry about that, Louis. I got three men: Lester, Country, and Reba's cousin Ewell from down in the boondocks. Don't worry, when men find out there's work, you'll have more than you need."

With that, a little union was formed especially when Abe Chlem saw the confab from across the street and came running. He joined in promising all the Jewish business. Dad was anxious to get started since the telephone had never stopped ringing and asked Frankie, "How the hell are you going to take tile to that house out East that you wanted to get started on this morning?"

Frankie smiled and without turning his head, hollered over his shoulder, "Lester, pull that car around back and you and Ewell load up the trunk. And don't forget the back seat."

The two filled the convertible with tile, from stem to stern, Lester bitching all the while about ruining his seat covers, then Frankie was ready to take off but only after promising to collect for his work that same day and bring payment by our house that afternoon. To Frankie's consternation, Dad pitched a little extra into the deal.

"Tell you what Frankie. How about you leave Ewell here to work with JoJo. There ain't no way that youngin' can last all day pulling up tile for Charley."

Frankie, anxious to get started finally agreed knowing he was probably going to get himself in trouble with Lester, not much good as a helper since he already had a buzz on. He was leaving his hardest worker Ewell who had done most of the loading and still had not said a word. Frankie and Lester drove off heading east on Poplar, the convertible bottom dragging the pavement as it went down Poplar, sparks flying from the tailpipe.

For the next couple of months Dad and Louis did more business and made more money than the company had made since the Depression had begun.

Every morning Dad would ask, as we drove to the shop, the same question, "JoJo, how much tile and slate have we got left back there in the shed?"

Of course I would make up some figure and when I told him, Dad would look over at Louis and grin. Everyone was feeling happy and prosperous. Ewell still left every afternoon and headed back to Reba's apartment but spent the day just as promised working with me doing the grunt work pulling up material then cleaning up after the job was finished.

Werner Sheet Metal for the first time in years was showing a profit, not only doing as much work as Dad could oversee, but selling materials to Chlem, Frankie and even some of the larger shops.

Most were working seven days a week, drinking up some of their wages each night, then sweating out the hangover the next day until the heat and tiresome work began to wear them down. Finally Dad had a bout with his old nemesis, rheumatism. For years he had suffered with leg swellings so badly and pain so severe that he lay in bed moaning with the smell of Ben-Gay permeating the house. Now, at the time when Werner was a making a real showing Dad was laid up, his only contact the telephone and me.

For the next three weeks Hank, the most reliable tinner of the crew would come by each morning and pick me up then Uncle Louis and head for the shop. No one was happy having a fourteen-year-old giving orders whether coming from the boss or not but Dad knew Hank would change things to suit himself and Louis would get too nervous so I solemnly gave out who was to go where and what to do while the men would give me the evil eye.

As Saturday approached it seemed that none of the men wanted to work but Werner had a very good customer, Winter Switch Company, owned and run by a son-of-a-bitch, or so the men said, by the name of Turner. Turner called Dad's bedside telephone on Friday demanding that we finish his roof over the weekend while his plant was closed and Dad, having no choice, agreed. With as strong a voice as a scared shitless fourteen-year-old can use I told Hank, Cal, and Black Robert that they would have to finish the job that next day. All three almost refused but seeing that it was going to ruin my day and that they would make overtime, they simply stared at me almost with glee.

But that Saturday was one of those days I would just as soon forget.

Hank picked me up and after he looked at Dad's swollen leg seemed to be a better mood, but boy, was he hung over. Then when we got to the job I could see that Black Robert and Cal were in no better shape, maybe even worse than Hank.

The job was to install tile and copper flashing atop a flat roof that beveled down forty feet or so, much like a ski slope. The Switch Company made parts for cotton gins and the roof was home to what seemed like half the pigeons of Memphis. As we climbed out onto the flat roof, the bird shit was so slippery that I almost fell off the roof and down the slope. Instead, I grabbed Cal who let out a yelp and pushed me away, promptly sliding into Black Robert. Within the hour, all four of us smelled badly enough to gag, the new copper and tile were covered with bird shit, and no one was speaking. The cussing was becoming louder, the three men gradually gathering together as one to blame me as if I were the culprit who had somehow caused the pigeons to roost and shit all over the roof.

After four hours or so Cal looked over at me as I was laying the copper in place for the three of them to attach to the roof and with a stare that warned me not to open my mouth, pulled out a pint of moonshine. The men who knew me were sure that I wouldn't snitch on them bosses son or not, but the way the threesome had treated me that day made me speak up.

"Don't y'all go getting' drunk now. That old man downstairs is mean as a snake. Ya'll know he is."

That shut everybody up for a while but I noticed that none of the three spoke to me and sure enough, all of them were starting to perk up going so far as to make fun of the pigeon shit starting to cover their clothes. Then for whatever reason, probably hearing all the cussing, and maybe because he really was a son-of-a-bitch, Mr. Turner came out of his office, shading his eyes and hollering, "What are you men doing, I'm paying good money for Werner to get this work done and all I hear is bad language. Please stop the curse words, get finished, and let me go home."

We were about finished with the job, all three of the men tight as a tick, everyone's clothes permeated with an awful smell, when Mr. Turner showed in the yard below. This time we could see that he was really mad, red in the face, hands on hips as he yelled, "It sounds to me as if you men are drunk. I'm going to report you to your boss."

Looking back, I figured that was all it took to bust them loose. The three of them acting as one began throwing pieces of tile, wood scraps, hell, even pigeon shit in clumps, at Mr. Turner as he dodged and ran back into his office. Luckily the moonshine had affected their aim and they never came close to hitting him.

We quickly finished the job and got the hell out of there. Hank was still sober enough to drive me home but when I walked in the front door, my smell leading the way, Dad yelled from his bed, "Come here JoJo," and when I reached his door, he asked, "What the hell happened? That son-of-a-bitch Turner called and he said everybody was drunk and not only that, they were throwing things at him."

And with that, Dad, bad leg and all almost grinned saying, "What the hell is that smell?"

Of course I lied, saying something to the effect that Turner just didn't like us and of course Dad didn't believe a damn word I said but probably felt sorry for me between putting up with three drunks and being covered in bird shit to boot.

The repair and replacement work continued for another three months gradually fading to a trickle but the freak storm, a disaster to insurance companies had helped many a business, Werner Sheet Metal included. I had gone back to school but still worked on Saturdays and when I rode in the back seat, I sat up straight not afraid for my buddies to hear Dad and Uncle Louis holler at each other anymore. Now they talked about things, like maybe, just maybe, buying a new truck.

Abe Chlem had done well for himself as always. Even Frankie and Reba had done well with Frankie doing the tile repair along with

Junior and Country and Reba handling the money, collecting for a job just as the last tile was laid. They had done well enough that they were able to move to a new location. It was a shop outside of the Skid Row area with their apartment located as before directly above the shop. Frankie fell in love with the place as soon as he saw it when he eyed a beer joint on the corner by the name of the Owl, a place that reminded him with fond memories of the Red Rose.

Frankie, still wishy-washy about getting another pickup had never even repaired the holes in the floor of the truck. He kept telling Reba, "Honey, it's almost summertime, them holes will cool the cab a lot better."

This was after Frankie had gone out with a drinking buddy, passed a used car lot and saw a yellow convertible, one just like Lester's. Not long before, Lester had been killed, done in by a big oak tree hitting it head-on when he was drunk missing a curve at sixty miles an hour.

Frankie told Reba, "Honey, I just had to buy that car. It brought tears to my eyes, reminding me of Lester every time I saw it."

Reba's cousin Ewell had stayed with Werner for the three months or so, just as Frankie had promised. Uncle Louis told Dad, when I was eavesdropping one afternoon saying, in a smug tone, "Shit Joe, you know why that Ewell boy is still here don't ya? Frankie already sees too much of him now, him living with them two, and him being Reba's kinfolk and all." Besides, Louis added, "Frankie can't sneak over to the Red Rose and catch that little waitress, like Hank said. Hell, he told me that Frankie was nailing her most every night."

For some reason that I would never understand, Ewell and I had become really close friends. We had worked together, side by side for over three months, pulling up tile and slate, while Charley, Hank, and Cal did the repairs. Then, when we had the roof stocked, the two of us helped in nailing down the tarpaper for the undercoating.

There was a large gulf in age between the two of us, but Ewell was a farm boy living far back in the boondocks with no friends raised by a father even less educated than his own son and innocent as a newborn lamb. I may have been a skinny fourteen-year-old but I had been around girls, knew where most all of the pieces were, and supposedly how they performed, and had kissed girls, admittedly when playing spin the bottle. So, as the months went by, a fourteen-year-old was giving sex education to a twenty-something-year-old.

In exchange, through some unwritten rule as if he felt in some way obligated, Ewell was doing most of the hard work, pulling on that damned rope all day long, lifting the tile or slate, seemingly tirelessly, always in a good mood, and not grouchy like me.

As the work slacked off and Ewell was headed back to Frankie's new shop, I began to realize just how much I was going to miss him. On the last day when the work had petered out and Ewell was leaving to go back to Frankie's shop, Ewell, no one for big words, grabbed me around the shoulders and said, "I sure hope we get to see each other again someday, JoJo."

For years a picture of Ewell or Junior would pop into my head. Like Junior, the young roofer's helper who ate lunch with me every day while sitting under a tree, I felt that I had missed a chance to form a special relationship. While Junior was an adult in a youngster's body, Ewell had the body of a grown man but still had the innocence of a teenager. They both possessed a kindness, an understanding of others, simple traits that I failed to find in people that I encountered in later life.

I never saw Junior or Ewell again. At times as the boss instead of a tinner and while inspecting the metal work on a roof, I would recognize members of the roofing crew who had worked alongside Junior and me. But when I inquired, the men would give me a glare seeing a boss in a tie, a guy they called 'The man' instead of a skinny little fourteen-year-old, then there would be a curt no or a simple shake of the head.

The idea that I had never done enough to locate Junior continued to hang over me like a Memphis cloud in the dead of winter, and on the spur of the moment when driving in the neighborhood one day, I decided to locate Junior's old house on Alabama Street.

As I parked, then walked up the broken concrete driveway, I was suddenly embarrassed, sure that the people in the shuttered old house would think that a grown white man, especially one wearing a necktie, must be bringing trouble.

After banging on the door, then knocking on a window pane until it rattled, a gaunt blind man dressed in ragged overalls opened the door only a crack, then stared with sightless eyes while an older black lady in a hand-me-down dress stood close behind, neither saying a word. And when I asked about Junior, I was met by the same grunts and a shake of the head as the roofing crew had done me. Though I tried to pry information from the twosome, somehow sure that this was Junior's parents, I saw only blank, grim-faced stares.

I left having accomplished little except scaring two old people half to death. I knew that I was left to live with emptiness and guilt. Feelings can nag at the edge of one's mind like a splinter stuck just below the skin.

I was on good terms with Reba, and once driving down Cooper Street, on a whim I stopped at her shop. Reba still lived in the apartment above the shop and swore that she counted the forty steps each day. Reba looked as pretty as ever but was having a tough go of it trying to run the shop by herself after Frankie had been killed, falling from a three story building. I wondered but didn't ask if Frankie was drunk at the time. After refusing help of any kind, Reba and I sat for hours reminiscing about the days on Skid Row while we had a few drinks. The new shop never took off the way she and Frankie thought it would even when building began to boom and projects popped up all over Memphis. Frankie just wasn't a businessman and had too much swagger to boot, often making a contractor mad and, of course, he had that famous temper often getting himself in Dutch, punching some other drunk out after having too much to drink at the corner bar.

Reba said, "JoJo, it got so Frankie was back in his old habits every Friday night even when I went with him so I could stop him from drinking too much." Reba continued, "It got that I spent many a Friday night at the lock-up downtown bailing out one or more of the tinners and once in a while, Frankie scooped up for being drunk." The nighttime jailer she said had even told her once, "Honey, you been here so many times, I know it's you by the sound of them high heels."

"So you see, JoJo, those dreams that I had didn't work out so well after all. I'm by myself and I'm still walking up forty steps."

Both of us had being sipping what Reba called her toddies and more than a little tight but still curious, I asked, "Reba, what in hell ever happened to Ewell?" And with the mention of that name, Reba's face lit up.

She talked and I listened as Reba, with more spunk than she had shown all day, related Ewell's story, one that took hours, along with a few more drinks, many smiles and a few tears.

15

Ewell As A Young Man

Ewell stood with his hands resting on the kitchen sink, looking out the window through the dirty panes, at the grey dust blowing across the hardscrabble ground that surrounded the place, shaking his head.

Now that his Daddy was gone Ewell was at a loss, not knowing where to turn. It was only last week when he came in for his lunch, a short walk from the saw mill where he worked that he found his Daddy dead, face down on the table, his untouched baloney sandwich in one hand, his nearly full glass of buttermilk in the other. The expression on the dead man's face was one of serenity, as if he were happy to be leaving this God forsaken world.

Ewell began working in the plant down the road when he was sixteen, not quite the legal age to work in a sawmill, but since he looked much older, and the foreman knew and liked his Daddy, he let the age situation slide. Meanwhile, his Daddy did a little cabinetwork on the side, his body to stove-up with rheumatism to work full time.

They had lived this way, just the two of them, since his Momma had run off with a drummer who was passing through town. The local gossip was that the drummer decided to stop at the local dive, a small, unpainted concrete block building, no larger than a decent sized kitchen, the roof covered with tar paper which lapped down the sides, attached with roofing nails and metal tabs, shaped like coke bottle tops.

A rusty tin sign, advertising Goldcrest 51 Beer hung at a bias on the front of the building, swinging to and fro in the breeze, as if it were an arm beckoning patrons to enter. The little joint had no windows, only a front door, with a screen hung partway open, as if welcoming all the blue bottle flies in the area. The place was as dark as a cloudy night, even during mid-day, a place too small to be called a honky-tonk, not even big enough to attract mean drunks.

While the drummer waited to wet his whistle before he headed for the next town some ten miles down the country road, he glanced to the end of the bar to where it curved, and there sat Ewell's Momma on a stool, having her afternoon beer.

As dark as the interior of the place was he couldn't be sure if the woman was young, old, ugly, or middling, most likely not too pretty if she was in this dive, but being a gambling man the drummer sidled down the bar, sure that he could get out the flappy door, and into his car, if the gal turned out to be a disaster.

The drummer had a gift for gab, and being a tad near sighted, not sure what he was looking at, he lit into his pitch. One thing led to another, the beer and the bullshit coming in equal amounts, and before long Ewell's Momma was in the front seat of the roadster, while the drummer's wares, those being parts for sewing machines, repositioned in the trunk. After having had a more than ample amount of beer the drummer, who was short and scruffy, with a stomach that resembled a bay window found Ewell's Momma both pretty, and anxious to get the hell out of town. Being a lonely man, with no one to talk to and he did love to talk, the woman, even though a little worn down at the heels was a welcome addition.

The way he saw it, through beer blurred eyes, the two could make a go of it as they traveled to the plants located all over the south, selling replacement parts for sewing machines. Plants where women in the small country towns had a chance to make some income by turning out denim pants, working long hours sewing parts together, being paid by the piece for each pair of pants they produced, since, in most cases their husbands had no job, and damned little chance of getting one.

Ewell had been just a kid when his Momma ran off with the drummer and remembered very little about her, only once, when he was ten he had received a postcard of an oily looking beach in Galveston, Texas, which read in childish round letters, "Dear Ewell, mind your Daddy, I miss you, Love Momma."

At the end of the message was a hand drawn heart with a smeared lipstick kiss, and for days Ewell would smell and touch the lipstick, wondering what his Momma looked like, and why she had left him, the kind of feeling that gave Ewell a stomach ache, and a sort of guilty feeling.

Ewell had little formal education, going only through the seventh grade. He had hated school while he was there, mostly getting into fights when one of the other kids called him a retard and a bastard. He wasn't sure what the words meant, but, since the boy snickered, and the other punks laughed, Ewell figured it was something bad, so he socked the kid in the mouth.

Because Ewell was large for his age and strong as a mule, the teaser at times ended up with a few less teeth or at least a busted nose while his teacher, Mrs. Davis, would keep Ewell after school. He would sit at his desk, his knees bumping the bottom writing, "I will not fight," over and over in his spiral notebook. By the time he finished his punishment and walked the two miles from school Ewell had little time to do chores, much less his homework.

Ewell became a big, raw boned man by the age of fifteen,

93

over six feet tall and strong as a bull, not handsome, but with strong features, a good chin, and a soothing manner that put others at ease. He knew nothing about women, having tried asking once, while being kept after school, writing in his notebook, "I will not fight," but when he asked Mrs. Davis about girl stuff, she turned a bright red saying, "Ewell, that's a question for your momma or your preacher."

Of course Ewell had neither, and by the seventh grade he was beginning to have funny feelings in his groin, especially in bed at night, so he went ahead and asked his only friend in class, a kid named Bud, the only boy nearly as big as Ewell, but a lot more citified, with sisters, and brothers, and mostly, a Momma. When Ewell asked him the same question that he had asked Mrs. Davis, Bud started getting red in the face, thinking maybe Ewell was making fun of him, then, seeing that Ewell was serious, sat down next to him, and speaking in a manner his Daddy might use, tried to explain.

"It starts by getting the girl all hot Ewell, you know kissing and feeling her titties and that kinda stuff. Then, when she starts turning red in the face you get her to pull up her dress, and take off her panties, then lay down on her back and spread her legs real wide." At that point Bud stopped, seeing that Ewell's mouth was hanging open. "This is the important part Ewell, so listen real good. Now real quick, before she cools off and changes her mind you pull off your pants, and lay down on top of her. That's when you put your thing in her and go back and forth real fast. Hell, Ewell," Bud explained, "It don't take but a minute."

Seeing the expression on Ewell's face, knowing that he didn't understand, Bud said, "Watch this Ewell." He touched his thumb and index finger together to make a small circle, then took the index finger on his other hand and ran it through the circle in a rapid motion, saying, "See Ewell, do it just like that."

Ewell stared in amazement saying, "Boy Bud, don't that hurt, seems like to me it would kill that poor girl." Bud, who lived closer to the little town, and knew all the girls from the wrong side of the tracks, sort of smirked and said, "Naw Ewell, I tried with Jo Ellen one time and she hollered like I was killin' her, but when I stopped she just grabbed me and pulled me back up on top. Man, girls are funny."

That night when Ewell was laying in bed and got that funny feeling in his groin he reached down and touched himself, then again and again until white stuff came flying out all over his hand. After that it was Katie bar the door, Ewell could hardly wait to go to bed at night.

16

Ewell Moves To The Big City

Ewell had failed the seventh grade and seemed to be making little progress in his learning, most likely to repeat the grade again and his Daddy going downhill fast, trying to work the lumber in the small cabinet shop there was no other choice than to do as his Daddy said one rainy afternoon, "Son, I done petered out, and you sure as hell don't need any more schooling. What'd you say if I asked you to lay down the pencil and paper and pick up a hammer?"

For the next few years Ewell and his Daddy existed on what little bit of money that could be scrounged up from making a few cabinets each month. There was an old country store within walking distance where they could buy the essentials: flour, bread, salt meat, and buttermilk.

The old man was a good shot, and when he was at himself hunted deer and rabbit. A large deer could last the two of them for a month, and Ewell became a wizard at cooking rabbit stew. Their day always started with a breakfast of oatmeal coated with honey, along with bread fried in the skillet, using lard and toasted until it was black.

They lived in a small wood-framed house with batten seams

covering the butted joints, roofed with ninety pound slate coat paper, sitting on concrete block pillars for a foundation and a falling down porch. In truth the house was not much more than a shack, but neither son nor Daddy seemed to pay much attention.

Life was in limbo for Ewell, a rut so deep that he lived by repetition, time meaning nothing, the largest adventure a trip to the little country store. There were days on end when father and son hardly spoke.

The place was on a gravel road, the land flat for miles in every direction and a wind that seemed to blow year round, keeping the yard coated with an ugly red dust.

As his Daddy became poorly Ewell applied for a job at the saw mill down the road, some mile or two away, the same mill that put out an odor of rotten eggs, the smell that he had lived with all of his life.

But now, there was a new kind of rut for Ewell. He would rise every morning at five o'clock and traipse down the road to work in the saw lumber all day, then come home late in the afternoon smelling of pine tar, eat his supper, sit in the same old chair for an hour or two, go to bed, and repeat the same dull routine the next day.

Ewell was not a dumb young man, maybe not educated, but had clarity about him. He could picture what he would become in twenty years if he stayed at the mill. He could feel himself shrinking, his smile less ready, and his mood more somber.

On just a few occasions did he have the gumption to go into Memphis some twenty miles away with a few of the other men, the ones who worked at the mill, most all of them much older. When he did, they would ride the broken down old bus into downtown, the redneck's dressed in bibbed overalls, with bandanas around their necks, and slicked back hair.

Somehow, surely without intention, the crew always ended

up drunk on moonshine, and, at some point, the fools would try to pick up a woman or end up in a fight, and, more than likely, end up in jail.

Ewell would leave the damn fools and go to a movie, where he would sit, lost in the quiet darkness of the theater, turning away from the cowboy pictures that his buddies went to see, movies with lots of shooting and Indians, instead opting for the more glamorous love stories. He could sit through two showings of a movie with Betty Davis or Carol Lombard on a Sunday afternoon, eat a bag of popcorn, then, all alone, never having a woman, except from the pictures in his mind, while lost in dreams as he sat in the dark theater, take the bus back to the place where it stopped at the gravel road, with his head filled with a week full of dreams.

Ewell's Daddy never mentioned his Momma but once, and that was when near the time when he dropped dead. A peddler, surely having a bad day, stopped by, trying to sell insurance, and figuring a pint of moonshine would loosen the old man's purse strings got his Daddy drunk, but the man left, mad as a wet hen when he found there was nothing in the old man's wallet but dust and lint. When Ewell came home that night his Dad was sprawled at the kitchen table, sound asleep. When he awoke, still drunk, he began crying and told Ewell about his Ma.

He said, "Son, I ain't gonna lie to you. Years ago, before she ran off with that drummer man she come home drunk. Sometimes when your Momma got drunk she got mean, and when we got in a fight and I knocked her upside the head. When she got off the floor, falling all over herself she spit at me and said you wasn't mine." Then the old man wobbled out to the steps, fell down the stairs, and lay on the ground crying, until Ewell picked him up and put him to bed.

Now, his Daddy was planted deep in the ground, right under a big old sycamore tree that he had loved, and for the first time in many years Ewell looked around at the sorry hovel he called home. He had almost no money after paying the funeral home and the preacher, and felt nothing but numbness.

Ewell, simply from habit, stuck with the saw mill, living alone, going into town once a month, regular as clockwork to have a good meal at the Cafeteria, the old one downtown that looked expensive, but wasn't, then to a double feature, one with a good love story. It was a sad, dreary, pointless, life.

Once in a blue moon, when the itch got under his skin, Ewell would pay a visit to Mulberry Street, where three shotgun houses stood. There, Ewell would slough against a wall, waiting his turn, for a two dollar roll, with a gal already laying on an old mattress, her legs spread wide, saying, "Come on boy. I ain't got all night."

Ewell could feel his young life slipping away, gnawing at him more and more as he lay in his lonely bed each night, until one day at the mill when a man working near him slid into a rotary blade and cut his arm off at the shoulder, the man's life sliding away, the blood spouting like a hose. That night Ewell drank a full pint of moonshine, unable to forget the picture of the life flowing from the stump, the blood covering the floor.

Things would probably have gone on for Ewell, his life style just as dull as old paint if the telephone hadn't run one night when he was eating his supper. He was on a party line with two other households so when his signal, the one with three rings, his rings, came through it was so rare he was sure it was a wrong number. He studied the telephone long enough for the noise to become bothersome for the people who were connected to his party line, then grabbed the receiver as if it were a hot potato.

"Hello, It's me, Ewell," he yelled.

"Hi Ewell, this is your cousin Reba, do you remember me at all." There was a complete silence, one that lasted so long Reba thought that Ewell may have hung up, but she continued. "I know it's been a long time, even since we were kids, but I'd like to talk to you."

Without giving Ewell a chance to answer Reba carried on, "You and me are the last of our family, could you come up here to Memphis for a visit."

And with that one call, a new life would begin for a young man who had gotten so little from his dreary, dull years. He couldn't remember Reba but she sounded so full of life, a voice that laughed when she talked even over the static from the old telephone. When he hung up, after telling Reba that he would be at the Greyhound Station the next weekend Ewell stood in a stupor, still holding the receiver in his big mitt. While tears ran down his face, and a flush reddened his cheeks, Ewell stood, until Miss Abbie, the old lady on the party line with only one ring, the one who listened in on everyone's conversation, began hollering, "Ewell, is that you, did I hear you say that you're gonna leave for Memphis."

17

Reba, Betty Jo And Hannah

"A deal is a deal Reba," Frankie said, as they lay in bed, a few weeks after Ewell had moved into their apartment, having brought his few belongings, and almost no money, from his trip down in the boondocks. "I told Joe and Louis that they could keep Ewell as a helper, until they got over the hump, and I mean to keep my word." Reba made a sound in her throat, turned in bed until she was as far away from Frankie as possible, then fretted all night.

So, for the next three months Ewell worked for Werner, alongside JoJo, the boss's son, as a helper, pulling up tile, and helping to repair the broken roofs, all over Memphis. Each night Ewell finished work then headed back to the apartment to eat and sleep.

But that was a thing of the past, and now Ewell was working with Frankie, learning the sheet metal trade. Reba loved the idea of having kinfolks. It made her feel as if there were continuity to life. Since she and Frankie couldn't have children, cousin Ewell though not the perfect substitute, did his best. Though he was only a few years younger than her Ewell was as innocent as a child. Now he lived in the small apartment with them, occupying a room directly next to their bedroom, one with paper-thin walls, causing embarrassment at times, Frankie being a somewhat noisy lover, especially after having too much to drink.

Frankie had a hard time adjusting to a grown man who didn't want a drink or two every night, or being single and nice looking to boot, refusing the high-steppers when they tried to make a pitch. It was enough to make him wonder that maybe Ewell might be, one of them things, until, at times when Frankie had gotten pretty rambunctious in bed the night before, at least from what he could remember Ewell would grab the first woman who made a hit on him and take off down the street.

Frankie used Ewell to become a part time helper in the sheet metal trade, and within a few months Ewell was already working with some of the men in the field, hanging gutter and downspout as well as many of the tinners who had been at the trade for years. Ewell loved the work, loved the excitement of climbing high up on an extension ladder, seeing the sky from forty feet, as he clung to the eave of a three-story building instead of the grey dust that swirled across the yard at his daddy's old farm.

And, as he became a better tinner, learning from the older men, he was becoming a little more like them, catching some of their bad habits, coming home late after having had a little too much to drink, and smelling of cheap toilet water. Reba loved Ewell, and she was determined that her one relative was not going to end up a tinner, with a hangover every day, running around with that bunch from the Red Rose, always going out with the wrong kind. She was going to find him a decent woman.

On a particularly bad Saturday morning, when Ewell's head felt like an overripe watermelon, a smell of cheap perfume permeating his clothes, Reba sat him down at the kitchen table. "Ewell," Reba said, "I've been talking to a good friend of mine, a girl that I grew up with. She lives down in Sardis, not but thirty miles away, down across the Mississippi line. Her name's Betty Jo,"

Reba went on, "And she's always telling me about this widow, a real nice Christian woman, and how she's awful young to be a widow."

Reba could see that Ewell was suffering, so, thinking that it was a good time to strike, while the iron was hot, continued, "I know that you've been running around with a lot of tough girls, and sooner or later, you're going to get yourself in trouble, tell you what, I'll go call Betty Jo."

After spending what seemed like a half days pay on long distance charges Reba broached the subject of the widow Hanna to her friend, "Betty Jo, didn't you say that this Hanna woman down the road was a widow."

Reba added, "You remember my cousin Ewell who's living here with us, he's about to drive us all crazy, if I don't get him married off pretty soon Frankie's going to get him in real trouble."

With no hesitation Betty Jo yelped, "Lord Reba, that girl would be perfect;" remembering the kind of thoughts that she had on some occasions at get-togethers, when she sidled up close to Ewell after she had one or two sips too many. If only that boy wasn't so dull she might have done more than sidle, remembering the way he was built just like the fullback on the high school team, the one that she had the hots for, even now getting warm between her legs as she hugged the telephone.

Reba could hear the heavy breathing, and knowing Betty Jo, had no doubts that her friend was lost in a another world, dreaming of that fullback of long ago, now that her husband Ronnie, had become like milk toast now-a-days, hell he even took the bible to bed with him.

Reba shouted loud enough to shake the telephone, "Betty Jo, are you going to daydream all day or help me, I've just got to do something or go crazy."

Betty Jo was her best friend, had been through childhood, left St. Thomas, and moved to Mississippi to attend high school, a somewhat faded beauty who had been homecoming queen, and after playing around for a while married Ronnie, a chunky looking guy from a wealthy family.

The two played hard, just the way that they had in school, living off the fat of the land until the Depression hit. Now they were living life in the hard times, wondering each year when the bank would reach out and take their farm, as they had all the others in the area, but for now Betty Jo and Ronnie survived well enough, both beginning to show signs of wear from the years of honky-tonking and hard living.

Recently, whether because of the Depression or more likely because he was just plain dumb, and a little tired Ronnie decided to get religion. He took the oath, quit drinking, never let his eyes wander the way they had in the past; Lord Reba could attest to that.

Now Ronnie was about to drive Betty Jo crazy, almost scary in the way that he had become so quiet, that is, unless you handed him a bible, at which time he would begin spouting verses at the top of his lungs. Hell, Reba thought, I used to like the way Ronnie flirted with me when he got lit, now, all I want to do is get away from him and back to Frankie.

Reba returned to the kitchen after arranging a time to meet Betty Jo and just in time to see Ewell opening the icebox to get a cold beer to help his hangover.

"All right Ewell, I'm going to Sardis tomorrow to Meet Betty Jo, and starting right this minute you better start laying off that beer."

The word passed on from Betty Jo by way of the local gossips was that Hanna's husband had been at the very least sixty-five, bent at the shoulders, like most men who stand behind a mule all day, and a hell raiser when he was young.

His momma whose husband had died years before, lived

with Hanna and John, her husband, was ninety or more, and a heavy churchgoer, Pentecostal being her reference, something Hanna had no truck with, but went to services every Wednesday night for two hours, and Sundays all day just to keep peace in the house. The hollering at the service was bad enough, giving her an awful headache, but when people began jumping up, speaking in tongues, then falling in fits on the floor, Hanna refused to attend and spent her time reading while John and momma-in-law passed their hours atoning for sins they most likely hadn't committed.

The rundown little house, where Hanna and momma-in-law lived with about forty acres of almost non-productive farmland was situated on a rutted dirt road, about a mile past Betty Jo and Ronnie, had only one bedroom, a tiny kitchen with a wood burning stove, sitting smack in the middle, a wraparound porch, and a one hole outhouse in the backyard.

From a distance the place had a desolate and abandoned look, but once a person got close to the house they could see none of the rusty car bodies, beer cans and spare tires lying around the yard. The old corrugated metal roof was starting to rust, and the house needed a paint job in the worst way. The thing the house really needed was a good, healthy man. According to Betty Jo, since the husband had been so much older than a young woman like Hanna, she nor any of the neighbors had the slightest idea why a smart, nice looking woman like Hanna traipsed off to marry a man old enough to be her father.

Of course, when country folks, just the same as city folks had no solid reason they invented one. Most common was the conclusion that Hanna got pregnant, the daddy left town, and the old man offered to take her in as his bride. There was no baby so the rumor soon started that she put the baby up for adoption.

Whatever the reason, Hanna and the old man and his momma all lived together always treating each other with respect,

Hanna quite often referring to her husband as Daddy.

About a year before, the old man had dropped dead while trying to pull up a stump, located smack in the middle of a cornfield that he was attempting to clear, and then cultivate. The old man was using a mule nearly as old as himself, attached with a chain on the root at one end and a leather strap, attached to the mule on the other.

Their only neighbor, who happened along the dusty old road told Hanna some time later that the mule, whose name was Hazel seemed to sag, then drop dead at the same time as the old man, just sort of lay gently next to her husband, who was already prone on the hard earth. For some strange reason the fool thought that the two of them rested like that every day so he kept going, rushing so as to not miss his lunch, since it would all gobbled up by those six kids of his.

Hanna found the two of them an hour later when she brought her husband his fried chicken and a jar of sweetened iced tea for his lunch. Hanna stood quietly for a while, not losing her composure, then ran and got her Momma-in-law. The old lady fell to her knees, and said prayers, then got overexcited for a while and spoke in tongues, while Hanna just stood, gritting her teeth, wondering what in the hell she was going to do now.

When the old lady had regained her senses the two of them commiserated for a lengthy time then decided to plant man and beast in that same spot, right next to each other, in the manner that they lay, just as they had worked together all these many years. The two went so far as to discuss whether it would feasible to leave the strap, still wrapped around the old man, attached to the mule's reins.

In the end, by planting the bodies just so, the rows would have a rounded spot in the middle, and for years to come the rows of corn would have a large bulge resembling a pregnant woman when it reached the makeshift grave of man and beast.

Hanna hired the boy of fifteen or so who sometimes helped out during harvest, and lived on the farm some quarter mile away to build a coffin from a piece of pine for her husband, but thought it far too expensive to build one for the mule. She then had the lad dig a grave for man and animal, side by side, a task that took a considerable length of time since it was a very large mule.

When the job was completed the man and beast had been planted six feet deep as required by both women, then Momma-in-law said words from the bible, the same kind of words that Hanna had no truck with.

After the burial, Hanna and Momma-in-law had a long debate before deciding to put a wooden cross at the head of each grave with the name of Hanna's husband, John on one and the name of the mule, Hazel on the other.

There were puzzling conversations among the town people when word got out, and snickering among the younger set, and there was a lengthy debate, a damned near argument, with the wood worker, who suggested a larger cross for the mule. In the end the crosses were made and placed just as the two women wished, and the wood worker muttered to himself that no one would ever believe him when he said he built a cross for a mule. As a last tribute the young man was instructed to find a number of nice big rocks, good round ones, and each a foot or so in diameter, set them in a circle in an orderly fashion, spaced just so, around the rounded graves, but before doing so Hanna had the youngster paint them white.

Reba told Betty Jo that they would meet the next afternoon in downtown Sardis at the only meeting place in town, a brand new Dairy Queen. Reba had insisted on meeting Hanna since she was not too sure that she could trust Betty Jo's judgments, what with her entertainment limited to church bring-a-plate socials. It would be just like her to set up some old gal who was ugly as homemade sin just to get some fun out of life.

Hanna had already heard the gossip since Betty Jo never could keep her mouth shut. She always had loved to be the center of attention. In a town as small as Sardis, with one caution light, which blinked yellow twenty four hours a day, seven days a week, a Pure Oil filling station, a combination hardware store and dress shop, and a Dairy Queen which served hamburgers, fries, and blizzards, a sort of soft malt that came in two flavors, chocolate, and vanilla. Hanna went to the Dairy Queen as often as possible, whether it was with her Momma-in-law or alone just to buy a blizzard, always requesting extra cream. She had heard the rumors which Betty Jo had planted knowing Hanna would pick them up from the local busybodys who spent much of the day at the Dairy Queen.

Hanna was a practical woman in her early-thirties, built without fat, with thick arms and sturdy legs. She kept her hair short, wore glasses on a roundish face, and when in her Sunday go-to-meeting clothes was attractive enough to turn a few heads. She was old enough to have experienced life, granted, a somewhat dull one, but not too sure if she wanted to jump into another marriage, especially with a city dude who probably wouldn't like her country ways. Momma-in-law was easy to get along with, she and Hanna never had a cross word, surely both knew how hard the marriage to John must have been for a young woman.

At times Hanna could stand at the little kitchen window and look out over the forty acres, which was now farmed by a sharecropper, a poor devil who had lost his land to the bank, a young guy with a passel of children and a bossy wife. If he noticed the crooked rows that went in a half circle around the graves of John and Hazel he never mentioned it, but Hanna remembered how little life had given to her and she would think to herself, "Lord, I don't need this, I've gone through thirty years and never really had much of a man, I reckon I can go the rest of the way by myself."

Hanna's little vegetable garden was directly behind the house, a place that was her haven, but there were times on hot summer days, when the heat invaded her whole body and mixed with the rich smell of fresh turned earth, and the sweat ran down her legs as she hoed the weeds in her garden, her sex would ache so badly that she would lift her dress and touch that certain spot, slowly and gently, until she reached a climax, then, with a sigh, let out a low moan and topple to the ground.

As she lay in a soft afterglow, with the damp earth touching her back and that special place throbbing with contentment, the heat from the noonday sun soaking her skin, her mind would wander, and she would think that maybe it wasn't too late for some sort of love after all.

Reba hated to drive even the short distance from Memphis to Sardis, she couldn't afford the gas money, and the ration stamps for the month were running out. But there was Betty Jo standing outside the Dairy Queen in shorts and a tiny halter, looking just like the cheerleader she had been, and even now fifteen years past high school still as pretty and shapely as ever.

"My, how things have changed," Reba thought sadly. "It was only yesterday that I would pick her up in front of a honky-tonk instead of a Dairy Queen."

Standing next to Betty Jo was Hanna, and Reba's first thought was: "Perfect." She had the heft and size for Ewell, and the way she stood, in a somewhat shy and awkward manner reminded her of Ewell's stance.

Reba jumped out of the old truck, ashamed for anyone to see the holes in the floor of the cab, began walking forward quickly, calling, "Hi Missy, I'm Reba, let's go get a blizzard, it's hot as hell out here."

The three went into the shop and found a booth in the rear

where they could talk and ordered, then after Reba kicked Betty Jo a couple of times to keep her quiet she explained, "Ewell needs a wife Hanna, someone strong and knowledgeable. He ain't never had many women before, or so he says, and from what Betty Jo tells me you've been married for quite some time so you ought to have had plenty of experience."

When no one said a word, Reba continued, "It seems to me you would fit the bill to a tee. What do you say to me getting my cousin down here and see how the two of you hit it off. I'll tell you right now he's bashful, but he ain't dumb and he's a good man. Truth be known he needs a woman in the worst way."

Hanna simply gawked. She had never met a person so outspoken before, but she liked Reba right off the bat. This slim little lady who stood no more than five feet tall, and had the shape of a model had driven up in a beat up half ton truck, and waltzed into the Dairy Queen, taking over like she owned the place; what a pleasure it was to have someone lay their cards on the table, without all that pussyfooting around, like them gossips around these parts.

"Miss Reba, I don't know what to say, I don't know what my Momma-in-law would say, and I don't know if I'm ready to give marriage a go again."

All three of the women knew that Hanna was sure as hell interested, Betty Jo and Reba could tell by simply looking at Hanna, wiggling her cute little butt in the seat, and the way she rubbed her hands up and down her crossed arms. Finally Betty Jo could stand it no longer, blurting out, "What the hell's wrong with you Hanna, don't waste the rest of your life with old people, surely you've had enough taking care of others."

The three sat for a while longer swirling the straw in their sodas, all the ice cream melted by now, hemming and hawing around, but by the time Reba pulled out on the highway headed back to Memphis, the old truck missing every third stroke, and a black plume coming from the exhaust pipe covering the asphalt, a deal had been struck. Reba would bring Ewell back to Sardis to meet Hanna the following Saturday.

18

Ewell And Hannah

It was still dark when Reba woke. This was going to be a big day, a good day hopefully, a day to remember fondly for a long time to come. She pulled herself from the warm bed and put her tiny feet on the wooden plank floor, the cold penetrating her whole body, her thin frame shivering in an old nightgown. She went to the window, the one that faced Cooper Street and gazed through the rattling windowpanes, the wind whistling around the windowsill.

Reba stared at the street below, where the black pavement glistened with the sheen from the rain, which covered its surface, the streetlight casting a yellow halo, the mist turning into drops as they disappeared from sight.

She turned to Frankie, still snoring from a bad Friday night hangover, and said, "I'll swear if I don't believe it's going to rain all day Frankie." Since there was no response, and none had been expected, and Reba knew that it was too early to get up she climbed back into bed, hardly waffling the springs and pulled the old duvet up to her chin. In an hour or so Reba would have to get herself back out of the warm bed, and somehow pull Frankie out of his whiskey soaked coma.

She thought to herself, "Frankie really tied one on last night, it seems as if he ties one on almost every night lately, and the more he drinks the more he looks for trouble. Something's got to give. Maybe, if Ewell hits it off with that woman Hanna we'll have some time to ourselves, maybe I can get him to straighten out."

Reba knew than when Frankie woke he would want an eye opener, and then another, and unless she put a cork in the bottle Frankie would be in no condition to drive a decent car, much less the beat-up old half ton Ford pickup sitting in the back lot. That old yellow convertible was long gone, turned in when they couldn't meet the payments.

The drive to Sardis wasn't that far, probably forty miles, but with the war on and since their gas stamps had just about run out for the month, and they couldn't afford to replace the thirty eight truck, nor the bald tires, nor the floorboards that had holes in them big enough for a size twelve shoe.

Reba had been after Frankie to fix the floorboards for months, but there was always an excuse, his men were too busy, the weather was so warm it gave off air to cool the cab. The excuses went on and on, much like Frankie's drinking: As the months went on and grew into years Reba had become both sad and frustrated.

As her thoughts of the whole mess made her more and more fidgety, much too anxious to sleep, Reba got out of the bed once more, pulled off her heavy bathrobe hanging from the hook on the back side of the bathroom door, slid her feet into her sturdy high heels and went down the forty steps counting them one by one as she did every morning, as if to remind herself that she didn't live on the hardscrabble dirt where she had raised as a child. As she descended, balancing herself on the handrail, she called to Ewell to get up and help fix breakfast.

But Ewell was already sitting at the breakfast table in his brand new go-to-meeting suit, hair freshly combed and Brylcreamed, his shoes shined, and a most woebegone expression on his face.

"Morning Reba," Ewell said, and took a sip of his long emptied cup.

"My god Ewell, how long have you been up?" Reba said as she worked her way around the table. As a show of affection, she ran her hands through his fluffed hair, making it a mess, knowing that his pompadour was the one thing Ewell was overly proud of.

"Do I really look right Reba?" Ewell said. "I feel like a barker at the mid-way, the ones that I used to see with Momma when I was a kid." And when he mentioned his mother he let out a torrent of sobs, crying being a fairly new thing for Ewell, started by the onset of newfound happiness, living with Frankie and Reba, and now with a new suit, and a woman to court.

To Ewell it was just all too much, the feeling that swarmed through his chest, a warm, unknown sensation that stretched across his heart, a shortness of breath when he thought of Hanna, and what might happen if the two of them hit it off.

Reba sat, with her first cup of coffee, filled with lots of cream and three heaping teaspoons of sugar, and watched Ewell. She was as proud as a mother hen. Though Ewell was only a few years younger than her his inexperience in women made her feel emotions that were new to her, almost bringing tears to her eyes. She saw how handsome he looked in his new suit, the one that she had spent an entire day shopping for, riding the streetcar downtown, walking carefully through all the department stores to check prices and sizes, then finding just the right price and size at Bond's, a nationwide Men's Store. It was a heavy wool suit, the checks possibly a little too bright, but the color bringing life to Ewell's somewhat hangdog face.

"Stand up Ewell, let me look at you," Reba said, and when he did Reba was beside herself.

"Ewell, you look just like a movie star that Hanna is going to fall all over herself for when she sees you."

With a glance at the wall clock Reba jumped, and headed for the stove, turning her head back, saying, "Come on, let's fix something to eat, then I'll wake Frankie."

While Ewell started cooking pancakes, his favorite, as long as they had plenty of Log Cabin syrup, Reba went upstairs to wake Frankie. Soon he could hear a commotion, and voices raised, mainly Frankie's, a sound like pleading, and soon a bouncing noise, one that he had become accustomed to over the last year, then quiet.

Ewell smiled as Reba came back down the stairs looking rumpled, trying to keep a straight face, and the noise of Frankie on the floor above whistling as he did every morning, hung over or not.

Frankie came downstairs shortly, clean shaven, dressed in a neat white shirt and sport coat, his ever present brown felt hat set at the same rakish angle. Ewell wondered how he could look chipper, having seen how drunk he was the night before, but before he could put the cooled off pancakes on the table Frankie said, "Reba, where's the good whiskey, the way my head feels from that rotgut last night I need an eye opener."

Frankie went to the cupboard standing in a corner of the tiny dining room, reached to the very back, and found a part bottle of Jim Beam, took a couple of big gulps right out of the bottle, belched, smiled, then returned the bottle to its hidey hole.

Sitting around the table soon became a somewhat tense situation, what with Frankie eyeing the cupboard, Ewell fidgeting in his chair and Reba glancing at the window, seeing the rain become heavier, spiting and crackling against the pane, making a dull noise like spent birdshot.

Breakfast finished, and the three bundled up as best they could, Reba decided to take things into her own hands after she had taken one look at Frankie sliding down the back steps, and a look at Ewell shaking his head, and shrugging his shoulders. As if to say, "It's all up to Reba, you know I don't know how to drive."

Reba sat at the wheel for the longest time, trying to get up her nerve, before finally cranking up the old motor, all the time cussing Frankie under her breath, knowing that she was a poor driver at the best of times, and a terrible driver on slick roads.

As the vehicle moved, it seemed to have a mind of its own, and as Reba held tight to the steering wheel, slid past the open gate skidding sideways until righting itself directly in the middle of Cooper Avenue. Driving slowly, but gaining confidence with every mile Reba drove down the old county road, afraid to be seen on the main highway and stopped by a state trooper since she had no driver's license, a drunk in the middle of the cab, and a man resembling both a side show barker and a madman riding shotgun.

The old truck trudged along the county road, the one with hardly any traffic, since anyone with good sense was using the main highway with its paved surface. The gravel road had become wet by now and Reba, wearing a new dress, high heels, and hose, while Ewell, in his new wool suit, and Frankie in his dress pants, were all beginning to feel the effects. As Reba looked down through the holes in the floorboards all she saw was brown water, much of it splashing onto her shoes, and looking across the sleeping Frankie at Ewell she could see his pants becoming soaked by that same brown rain water.

The gravel was getting worse, beginning to have more of a mud texture to it, as if the county had run out of funds, and Reba was at the point of crying, the one thing that she never did, when she looked up from the road and saw a grain silo in the distance, one that she knew to be close to Hanna's house.

Another half mile and there was the little lane that led to Hanna's, and Reba stepped on the gas, trying to goose the truck into going faster, but when the Ford made the turn it decided to just sit down like an old mule that had too much put on it for one day.

Frankie, who had been playing possum for the last hour, not wanting to drive, but wanting a drink, jumped up, hollering at Reba, "What the hell did you do that for, now we're going to have to walk."

For a few minutes the three just sat, Reba's famous temper about to erupt, Frankie wanting a drink, and Ewell starting to get scared, when Reba righted herself and ordered Ewell out of the truck. "Go on ahead Ewell, the house is right over yonder. Frankie and I will come on behind, there's no use in all of us showing up at the same time, it might be embarrassing."

Ewell knew that there was no use in arguing with Reba when she had that look, so he got out and took off across down the path when he heard Reba scream, "What the hell have you done to yourself, your pants are halfway up your leg," and looking down Ewell could see that the cheap wool suit had shrunk a good six inches. He stood in bewilderment as Reba took off her high heels, tossed them on the seat of the truck and jumped down onto the scratchy gravel, stinging her bare feet, but too damned mad to care, calling,

"Go on Ewell, it's too late to worry about what you look like now, we're already late as it is."

As Reba and Frankie followed behind, all she could think of was, "My God, I spent all that money to make Ewell look like a city boy, and now he looks more like a country hick than ever."

Somehow the three arrived at the front porch, Ewell leading the way, almost loping, gradually leaving Frankie and Reba behind, Frankie walking easy in his good boots, and Reba trying to tread lightly as the gravel began to hurt her bare feet. Ewell reached the front porch just as Hanna's momma-in-law came out the door, she surely had been watching through a crack in the wall for their arrival.

Ewell looked up with a smile that he had practiced for some

time when he noticed momma-in-law, instead of returning the grin, had turned her head and was scowling at a dark looking man leaning against a post not ten feet from where she stood.

By the time Reba and Frankie arrived Ewell had gained his senses, said, "How do, Ma'am," to momma-in-law, and turned to greet the stranger, who chose that moment to spit a long string of tobacco at a one eyed rooster who was idly scratching for God knows what in the gravel. The stranger's spurt missed by a good yard, and, seemingly a little miffed, as if they somehow had caused his poor aim, turned to meet the threesome.

Before momma-in-law could speak the stranger said, "Howdy folks, my name's Claude, and before Hanna's momma-in-law runs me off I just want you to know that I came over to put my two cents worth in for Hanna's hand but so far, I ain't even got her to come to the door to greet me."

With that said Claude, who obviously didn't have much hope to begin with, turned and tried again to spit at the old rooster and missed by again by a goodly measure.

It was such a querulous thing for a man to do, especially one courting a woman that Frankie asked, "What the hell are you trying to spit tobacco juice on that old rooster for, he don't look like he's doing anybody any harm."

"Aw hell Mac, I been spitting at that rooster every time I pass here hoping that Hanna would notice me. I live right down the road with my momma too, and it sure gets lonesome. When I heard she was getting courted I thought I might give it a shot. I don't mean no harm."

Reba looked at the farmer, a clean sort, with freshly washed overalls and a starched white shirt, and thought, "Mister, you don't know the first damned thing about courting if you think spitting tobacco at a rooster is gonna get a girl's attention."

Momma-in-law who had never said a word, just looking from

one person to another finally shook her head and offered, "I guess you're the one called Ewell, the one in the pants halfway up his legs, am I right." And when Ewell answered in the affirmative she said, "Well, Hanna's in the front room waiting on you, while you go calling I'll bring out some lemonade for the rest of us so you two can have some privacy."

While Ewell passed into the front parlor and out of earshot momma-in-law asked Reba, "How long has that boy had those pants, it looks to me like he's out growed 'em, I think I've got some old pants of daddy's in the closet that might fit him, I'll hunt around when I get the lemonade." Reba, being far too embarrassed to admit what had happened changed the subject to some everyday matter, something about the weather, while Frankie stood to one side staring at Claude, but watching him closely enough to see a pint of whiskey sticking out of his back pocket.

While the women were talking nonsense Frankie sidled up to Claude, saying. "Is that a bottle of what I think it is boy," and Claude trying to be polite, but scared to death of momma-in-law leaned over and quietly said, "yes sir, but don't let her know," pointing down the porch, he said, "She'd run me all the way out of her yard if she seen me with a bottle."

The group on the porch could hear murmuring from the parlor, and Frankie could see that Reba was keeping momma-in-law occupied, in order to give the lovers a chance to talk, so he gave Claude a sliding eye sort of look, and said, "I never tried chewing since I was a kid, How about giving me a chaw. Let me see if I can hit that one eyed devil, and while you're at it you might sneak me a sip from that bottle in your back pocket."

When Claude looked at the city slicker, with his fancy clothes, and his hat sitting on the side of his head, like some sort of big shot, asking for a chaw and a nip he figured that maybe the day that started so miserably wouldn't turn out so badly after all, if he could just talk this stranger into a spitting contest he might at least win a little money, after all it never had been his idea to court Hanna, the whole scheme had started by his momma.

Checking to be sure that Reba and momma-in-law had gone inside to the kitchen to get their lemonade, and maybe listen in a little on Ewell and Hanna, he said, "I'll tell you what mister, I'll bet you a quarter that I can hit that old rooster in his good eye with a shot of tobacco, and every time I miss I'll throw in a nip off my bottle."

Frankie, having seen Claude's marksmanship earlier in the day, and a mouth dry as cotton said, "Let's get to it buddy."

Within a short while both had a big lump in their jaw, the tobacco was flying and the rooster was dodging all over the yard, until the one eyed devil decided that the best tactic was to simply stand still, since neither one of the fools came within two feet of hitting him.

Ewell was a good man. He had never expected much out of life and that's all life had given him. When he walked into the room and first saw Hanna he felt a lurch in his chest, a feeling so intense that for a moment he almost lost his balance. There she sat, as wholesome and fine looking as he had hoped, a full figured woman, with bumps and swellings in all the right places. The little speech he had prepared, practiced for hours the night before was gone, his mind a blank, and as he opened his mouth nothing came out, instead with a voice as sweet as honey Hanna stood and said, "Hi Ewell, come over here and sit down, some folks went to a lot of trouble for us to meet, so let's don't disappoint them too much."

As she spoke Hanna was giving Ewell the once over. She liked what she saw. He was just the right height for a woman her size, had a nice build and really pretty hair, and he was well kept, but, she thought, if we were to get together I'll have to do something about those clothes, they are about four sizes too small.

Ewell sat while Hanna fixed some sweet tea, then sat next to Ewell, and all of a sudden Ewell relaxed and found his voice.

"Miss Hanna," he said, "I'm ain't much at talking to people, never did have a chance with no momma, and a daddy who didn't speak ten words a year. I don't have much education, but I've read a lot of books, mostly Westerns, and I'm a hard worker." With that Ewell took a large gulp of breath and continued, "Miss Hanna, I'm a plain spoken man, and the only way I know is to lay my cards on the table. If you'll have me I sure would like to start courting you."

Hanna sat quietly, looking steadily at Ewell, and thinking to herself, "Here's a man who sounds just like me, I had a good man for a husband, but he was more like a father, and I've got a good momma-in-law, but if she doesn't talk about Church, and being saved she doesn't talk at all. I know one thing for sure, I need a man in the worst way."

And without another thought Hanna said, "Ewell, I'd be delighted to have you calling any time that you wish."

With that one half hour two lonely people who had missed so much in life made the first step toward grabbing some of the happiness they had missed. They were good people, still young yet, and they would have to take just little steps at a time. Their love would grow, making bigger and bigger strides until the two would become like one, and their life together would be complete.

The evening was coming to a close. Ewell and Hanna left the sofa and came out on the porch. Ewell, with his hand in an awkward embrace on Hanna's back, afraid that somehow she may get away. Everyone was gathering on the porch, a chill was in the air, a mist rising around the group, and there was a silence that lay like a gentle blanket, but not unpleasant, more a feeling of contentment passing from one of the group to the other.

Claude and Frankie had given up trying to spit on the one eyed rooster, who now pecked contentedly at the bare gravel, while the two had split the bottle of moonshine. Claude had enough gas at his farm to fill the truck. Now they were the best of buddies, not drunk, but sure as hell not sober, just at a point that gave each a glow.

Momma-in-law was happy for Hanna; she had known for a long time that a man was needed in the house.

Reba felt sadness in losing her only kin, but she knew that Sardis wasn't that far away, and felt proud as a mother hen when she saw the gleam in Ewell's eyes.

In the years ahead, Ewell and Hanna would get married and take over the farm that lay dormant, the young man with all the kids having decided to take his family to Texas and try his hand at wildcatting. Ewell would buy a young mule, one just as slow and just as ornery as Hazel and would find that he was a natural born farmer. He would plant corn and cotton, and he would learn the proper method to plow around the pregnant graves.

And if he thought it unusual to find two crosses in the middle of a cotton field, he kept it to himself.

19

The Manor Next Door—A Grand Old Lady

A gravel driveway stood adjacent to the Werner Shop, the driveway then emptied into a back yard filled with slate, tile, scrap iron, and empty whisky bottles. The yard was surrounded by a wire fence, with a swinging gate, a lock that was rarely used, after all who would want to steal empty whiskey bottles, scrap metal, or old tile. The whole thing was topped with a coil of barbed wire.

Next to the gravel was forty feet of hardscrabble dirt with a few weeds pushing through cracks in soil tough enough to break a pickaxe. Past the weedy lot stood what was once a home, now a ramshackle old apartment, large enough to almost, but not quite be called a mansion. The dwelling, with its lack of upkeep had begun to squat, yet still showed signs of earlier grandeur, featuring four large columns, spread evenly across the wide front porch, reaching up thirty feet to support the ceiling, with its gabled roof, and ornamental fascia. The columns had begun to tilt, and the porch was beginning to lean. The huge house, named The Manor by the locals, was like a grand old lady, her strength gone, ready to give up, to possibly swoon, leaning toward the adjacent building, as if seeking support from the wall of its neighbor, Nick's Café.

Abe Chlem, whose shop was directly across the street, and knew about such things, stated, in no uncertain terms that the owners had, like so many unfortunates during the Depression, lost everything, including their residence. The bank in an effort to collect enough rent to pay the taxes allowed Mrs. Monroe to live rent free, acting as the apartment super. However, all the residents, and street people, knew her as a former madam, known only as Gertie.

Gertie had never been a madam, simply a former prostitute, grown old and weary, not cut out for the life anymore. However, she liked the title of Madam; it had a certain ring of authority to it, so she simply never corrected the folks who had put her in charge.

"Hell," she thought, "I ain't been called Mrs. Monroe in years."

Gertie paid her way by collecting the rent, keeping the house clean, watching the children while their Mommas, all high class prostitutes-known to everyone as high steppers, were away, plying their trade and making sure that no roughneck girls, or round heels, were allowed to live in the residence.

Uncle Louis knew all about the Manor, had known the former owners, and chatted up the young women up as they passed by each day, and they in turn loved talking to my Uncle. His blind eyes would bat furiously at the sound of high heels, walking at a prissy gait, when one of the young ladies, who would then stop to pass the time of day, before heading downtown to do their business.

Louis knew all by their names, and swore that he could tell by the sound of heels hitting the sidewalk and the smell of perfume, just who the girl was. Louis loved to reminisce about the good old days, before he was blind, and often bragged about the fact that he had been a rounder himself.

At the age of fifteen, and a kid who had barely gotten past first base, I was the perfect foil. Louis talked on and on, bragging in a soft tone that he was sure from the scent, that he had bedded one or more of the young ladies. As he mouthed what I thought was bullshit, I worked at a bench facing the Manor, watching with dried mouth, as the young women, half naked, slowly undressed before their bedroom window, leaving the drapes open, surely knowing that the kid next door would get an eye full.

20

Gertie and Crow, Part I

Gertie was a real high stepper in her heyday, a looker, legs long as fence posts that would knock your eyes out as she did the Charleston, in sequined, see through dresses that barely reached her mid-thigh.

She had lived in Chicago, had begun to party at the age of sixteen, and swore that she had gone to bed with all the big shots, from Al Capone to the Mayor of the city. But Gertie's luck ran out when she fell in love with a guy. The gent was tall, and handsome, with slicked back hair, and a mustache, a striking image of the movie star Douglas Fairbanks.

He swore that he was a graduate from an Ivy League School, and probably was, but unfortunately, Gertie's romance didn't last long. The John turned out to be a drunk and a lousy gambler.

Between the crap games, and the Depression, when his family lost all their money in the stock market crash, Gertie was soon out on the street.

She had been promised a goodly sum of greenbacks by her lover, money he had borrowed from Gertie during a dry spell when the cards had turned on him but the gent had disappeared, the money almost all gone.

Gertie, like all of her old gang was starting to sag, just too many long nights, too much booze, and too many guys. She was soon booted out of her place, and had just enough money to head south on the train headed to New Orleans, but when the money ran out she jumped the train, which by chance, happened to be in stopped in Memphis.

Gertie liked what she saw, especially a hangout by the name of the Green Beatle, a dive, but a real hot spot for all the locals, and located near the train station, but soon found that she was over the hill, even in this slow moving southern town, just plain outclassed, and, over a short period of time, she gravitated to Skid Row.

Gertie loved being called "the super." It had a name with authority attached to it. However, all she did was collect the rent, which she turned over, at the end of each month, to a young man, dressed in a boiled starched white dress shirt, with a clip on bow tie.

When talking to her tenants, she did her best to use high class words, words that she had heard from her long, lost lover, the kind that he had whispered into her ear after a particularly rambunctious roll in the hay. Gertie was pretty sure that the words were poetry, and felt flattered, even though the guy was drunk, so she stored those tidbits in her memory bank.

Gertie used caution when she taught the children, using those same high class words that sounded like poetry as they rolled off her tongue, the ones that had such a pretty sound, and the children in turn used the words when speaking with their mother, who in turn used the words with the Johns, during their lovemaking, in the hope that the bum would turn loose a little extra change. In some cases it worked, the dope thinking, "Damn, I done gone to bed with one of them gals that went to college."

Gertie took her job as babysitter, housemother, and

manager of the Manor seriously, seeing that the place stayed clean, the women neat and dressed properly before taking the trolley to Main Street, where they spent some of the afternoon, and most of the evening, perched ladylike, on a stool at Hazel's, a nice, quiet, upscale bar. And if the pickings were slim, the women might cross the street to Frank's Hotel, to lounge in a primly manner, waiting for a well off John to happen by, like what he saw, and make use of the rooms upstairs.

Gertie was as strict as a housemother with the women, allowing only the cream of the crop, the high steppers, the women with class. In addition, Gertie had a hard and fast rule that no man step foot on what she had come to believe was her realm, a world she would rule with a firm hand, as if she were their queen.

Unfortunately, Gertie didn't resemble a queen. Once, years before, she may have had the looks and shape of Mae West, but, over time her body had begun to squat, her breasts sagged as she gained weight, and, if one looked closely it was evident that she was beginning to grow a mustache. Gertie was oblivious to the change, still wearing dresses much too short for her tree trunk legs, with fake hose purchased in a bargain basement at a downtown department store, and her stringy hair, dyed orange, with lipstick, heavily applied, in a color to match her hair.

21

Gertie And Crow, Part II

Gertie had taken up with a former client when a wannabe pimp stopped in front of the apartment one afternoon, demanding to see one of the girls. The pimply faced tough showed up in a 1936 Model T, with busted springs, and bald tires, the crate squatting so low it almost touched the pavement.

"Where's Sissie?" the wannabe pimp hollered, "I got her a hot date lined up downtown, the bozo's ready, hell, he promised me two dollars on delivery."

Gertie took one look at the longhaired, dirty street kid and knew she would never let one of her girls go anywhere with him. The punk looked as if he hadn't bathed in a month, wore clothes that had seen better days, and when he opened his mouth, showed a missing tooth, something Gertie could never abide. Without looking, she began walking back toward the house, hollering over her shoulder, "Sissie ain't goin' nowhere with you boy so just get the hell out of here."

The pimp took one look at the squat bodied woman with orange hair, glanced around at the glassy eyed street people, and decided to go into the Manor and get Sissie, knowing there was no danger from any of the dull eyed bunch standing around with their heads hanging low.

The boy got out of his broken down heap, reaching into his back pocket for his switchblade knife, snapping it open as he started for Gertie, when an arm, with biceps as big as a blacksmith, and hands like sledge hammers, reached around the boy's waist, picked him up, and slammed him onto the hood of his jalopy.

And there stood Crow, in a leather apron, gazing down at the bloody kid, his nose pushed to one side of his face, blood pouring from a broken mouth, crying like a child. No one moved as the would-have-been pimp staggered to his car and took off as fast as the old crate would go, the bottom hitting every pothole, sparks flying as he flew over the hill in the distance. With that one gallant gesture Gertie wondered to herself if she was falling in love with that huge, bushy haired lug.

Gertie had known Crow for a while, having bedded down with him many times. Crow was married to a mad woman, who would disappear for days at a time, then show up with a pint of moonshine in her hand, and stand in the middle of the Poplar, screaming at the top of her lungs that she would never climb into their bed, until he came across with a quarter.

Since Crow's wife was ugly as homemade sin, hair frizzled in all directions, never washed, and had legs covered with large carbuncles, Crow decided the two dollars Gertie charged was a bargain. Crow owned a shoe repair shop cattycorner from the Manor, and, over time, he and Gertie had become friends as well as lovers. It did get on her nerves a little when Crow, who drank a full fifth of whiskey every day, began preaching the Gospel according to Lenin, especially while Gertie cuddled in his arms after one of their set-to's.

As the Depression deepened, and people became more desperate, Crow could often be seen standing at his shop door, bottle in hand, damning the United States for all the world's troubles, usually attracting a crowd of down-and-outers, wondering what the hell the crazy son-of-a-bitch was talking about.

But it began to worry Gertie when Crow, dressed in a neat black suit, a bright red tie, and bowler hat pressed tightly to his forehead, decided to take his cause to Court Square. The Square was located downtown, a gathering place for malcontents, crazy men or women, hair frizzled, clothes draped on sagging bodies, the kind of folks who marched to a different drummer.

Crow would be there every Saturday morning, right in the middle of that bunch, standing on a sturdy box, preaching in a deep baritone voice, loud enough to drown out all the others, shouting out his own brand of Bolshevik prattle. It mattered little to Gertie, thinking that it was only whiskey talking, but once, when she decided to tag along, wondering what all the fuss was about, Gertie became frightened. Crow was becoming more rabid in his speech, whipping the crowd into a frenzy, shouting for the overthrow of the Government, hollering slogans from books that he had brought from Russia, with quotes that he only half understood, and the mass of street people understood not at all.

Then, on a bright spring Saturday morning, as Crow was in the mist of one of his tirades, came a horde of horses, ridden by policemen in helmets, with night sticks in clenched fist, charging into the crowd, busting heads as they made their way toward Crow and the other speakers. The crowd scattered in all directions, most just wanting to miss a knot on the head from a policeman's baton; after all, to them this was only a diversion, a way to forget, just for one morning a week about their hunger, and the hunger of their wife and kids at home.

But Gertie could see the fury in Crow's eyes and she was afraid of what was going to happen to someone that she had found, someone who would take care of her. Gertie had seen the same scene when she lived in Chicago, that time, years ago, when the Reds had attempted to organize a union for the meat packers, and the Irish had done the same in the construction trade.

Gertie had seen the busted heads from batons, and sometime bullets flying from the police on horseback, and soldiers from the National Guard, as they charged the mob. She had seen that the blood, and in some cases, bodies, and she knew that Crow was fighting for a lost cause.

At times, Gertie had broached the idea, as they cuddled, of the two of them leaving Memphis, and Skid Row, heading for California, where Crow had heard of a Mexican, a guy by the name of Chavez, who was trying to organize the fruit pickers. Gertie thought, "Maybe Crow and me could start a new life together."

22

Sissie And The Peach Tree

Gertie's girls were a handful. The would-be-pimp who Crow had knocked silly was just one of the men problems that she dealt most every day. There were three classy looking women living at the Manor, and, at times, she felt as if she needed a shotgun to run off the riffraff who were like dogs in heat, sniffing around, waiting, hoping, for a chance to go out with a real dame.

Sissie saw the pimp drive up to the Manor in his old crate, as she and her friend sat at the second story window. She and Norma Jean shared a bedroom, the two of them gossiping when they heard the yelling, looked out the window, and saw the way that Gertie protected her, the way that big Russian knocked the shit out of the stupid kid, the bum thinking she was some kind of bimbo, probably thinking he could get her to crawl onto one of those filthy mattresses over at the flophouse, where he only paid the old man that ran the place fifty cents for an hour.

Sissie was tough as a dime steak. The two women who lived in the Manor knew little about her, a sort of unwritten rule, best to leave their past behind, when they became high class prostitutes. Gertie had seen Sissie on a corner downtown, and knew that she was turning tricks. Gertie stood in a doorway and watched the young girl, a tall one she thought with a willowy side to her, a pretty face but maybe a little too oval in shape.

Gertie had seen something of herself in Sissie, an attitude, one that said that she could take care of herself. Gertie needed another girl or two in the Manor, and jaywalked across the street, standing next to Sissie, just as she was running a bum off, with the simple wave of her hand.

"You handled that pretty well girl, you been at it long?" Gertie asked. Sissie looked at the older woman, the one with orange hair, frowned, and said, "Long enough, something I can help you with, sister."

It didn't take but a short while. Gertie asked Sissie to have a cup of coffee in the little café across the street, then squeezed herself into a booth too tight, and made small talk for a few minutes, before explaining a suspicious Sissie that she was looking for three high priced girls to live at the Manor.

"I ain't looking to make anything Sissie, just want you to pitch in and pay part of the rent, as long as you keep your business away from the place, and don't deal with pimps, booze, or drugs," Gertie said.

The offer was too good, and Sissie said so. "Lady, what's your take off of this, I ain't paying no woman pimp," but was soon soothed by Gertie when she said, "All I want is enough to pay the rent, I ain't a working girl no more."

It didn't take but a minute to clean out Sissie's clothes from her room, and the two of them traipsed down to the Manor. Over time Gertie and Sissie had become like mother and daughter.

Sissie was a North Memphis girl, from an area filled with shoe making plants, sweat shops that produced overalls—the cheap kind—and steel warehouses. She, her Mama and older brother Benny lived in a shotgun house, like the one next door, and the one after that, only a short distance from a sludge ditch, then an embankment, covered with grey gravel, that had a funky smell, leading to rattling rail tracks.

Trains shook the little house all day, and all night, at times making the dishes play a tap dance. It was probably the sorriest neighborhood in a city that had been filled with the poor before the Depression, and people who now had given up hope.

Sissie never knew her daddy. He was dead she before she was old enough to know him, but Benny, her older brother said he was a good man, just the careless type, falling off a roof that he was shingling, while he was walking the ridge line, sliding down the roof head first, landing on his neck, and dying right there on the spot.

Within a year her momma had taken up with Chester, a no account, who Sissie hated. Once, when in her cups, Sissie told Gertie, "I never had nothin', except Benny, and a peach tree he planted for me, and I'll never forget either one of them."

Benny had always looked out for her since she was a little thing, when Chester had moved into the house with their mama. When the old man got drunk and began eyeing Sissie, Benny would cut his eyes at him, giving Chester a stare, one that would scare the hell out of a copperhead, making sure he got the message.

Benny was the one who planted the peach tree for Sissie when she was only five years old. Sissie had never seen anything grow, until one day Benny brought home a sapling. God knows where he got it, probably stolen from some nursery. It was only two feet tall when Benny planted it. He almost broke a shovel in the hardscrabble dirt, digging the hole deeper than it need be then putting loose moss in the bottom.

Then Sissie watered the sick little twig every day, and, over time it blossomed into a beautiful tree, the only living piece of greenery in a grassless yard, the only thing of beauty in the whole neighborhood. Sissie watched as the tree grew, and finally began to bear fruit, too small to eat, picked to ruin by the blackbirds, even as Sissie threw rocks in a futile effort to chase the birds away.

When Sissie was ten, a growing girl, tall for her age, with long hair which curled at the bottom, and so blond the kids on her street nicknamed her towhead, the summer came and Sissie saw peaches, not just the little bird feed type, but big, round, juicy looking peaches, almost ready for picking.

Sissie hollered for Benny, wanting him to see, maybe help her up to the bottom branch, where she could scoot among the limbs, just get a look at something alive. But Benny was gone, as usual, having grown into a big tough, a thug, running with a gang, standing around at one of the corner joints, looking for trouble and usually finding it, and her Momma was working at the mill, like she did five days a week, doing twelve hour shifts.

As she stared up at the trunk, trying to figure out how to reach a branch she felt a movement behind her, and then a hand resting on her thigh, the smell of sweat and booze overpowering, as Chester said, "Here, Honey, let me help you up," and without warning reached beneath her dress and grabbed the cheeks of her ass.

Sissie didn't know what to do. She knew his callused hands hurt the way that they dug into her flesh and she knew that Benny had warned her to stay away from the old bastard when he was drunk but by now he had her about the waist, had pulled her down on the dusty ground and was tearing her white cotton panties off.

The old fool was grunting, like a rutting hog, trying to gets his pants down, but Sissie was strong and Chester was too drunk to hold her as she squirmed loose, sliding out from the smell of booze and sweat, then running, running, to the corner where Benny usually stood, slouched against a wall.

But Benny was gone, and Sissie was alone, so she picked up a bunch of rocks, when running back to the house, ready to kill that old man. When she rounded the corner, Chester was sprawled on the dirt, arms flayed out, his pants pulled down, snoring up a storm.

That night, when her Mama came home and Sissie told her what had taken place, her Mama picked up a switch and started after Sissie, saying, "What the hell's wrong with you girl, there's a devil in you, just stay away from Chester when he's drunk, instead of teasing him with your wanton ways."

That's the way it was with her momma after she got religion, even though she laid up with a no good, shiftless drunk, working all kind of hours, just to keep him in booze. Momma had been about as bad as Chester, until a former drinking friend, Della by name, talked her into going to the Pentecostal church a couple of blocks away, where she heard that preacher with the wiry hair, wearing all black clothes, hanging on a body built like a question mark, scared the hell out of her with his fire and brimstone sermon.

Then her getting dunked until she damned near drowned, coming up spitting a half gallon of dirty water, knowing she would never touch whiskey again, that she was gonna save Chester, stop Benny from running with that bunch of thugs, and keep that smart ass little Sissie from whoring around.

Then Sissie thought of that day, her birthday, the very day that she had turned fourteen, when her Mama was gone to work at the sewing mill, and Chester was drunk again.

As Sissie walked into the house Chester started in on her again, and Sissie ran as the fool chased her out the patched up screen door, stumbling down the steps, then how Sissie had climbed that peach tree, with Chester grabbing at her legs, but her too quick for him, pulling her feet into the branches. The way he tried to sweet talk her, but Sissie shaking her head all the time. Then him hollering, "Come on down here girl, I ain't gonna hurt you." But she knew, just like it would be just as it had been before, and she climbed higher, higher than she ever been, and the old drunk started after her, trying to get purchase on the trunk of that peach tree.

Sissie looked around and all she saw were peaches everywhere, and she grabbed a handful and threw, with an arm that had always been strong, right at Chester's head, and by God she hit him, over and over until he lost his balance, fell backward and landed on his head, with a sound like a cracked watermelon.

Sissie figured she must of kilt Chester, the way he just lay there, but the next thing she knew, her big brother Benny had the old man by the scruff of the neck, and was beating the tar out of him, and Sissie, scared that Benny was gonna kill that old drunk, scaled back down that peach tree, and she grabbed Benny, pulling with all her might, but Benny had just gone crazy, his eyes red as fire, the way he got sometimes.

And Sissie ran to the tap on the wall, filled a bucket with cold water, raced back to them two on the ground, and poured that cold water all over Benny's head. When it was all over with, Chester was a mess trying to squirm away, his face a pulp, covered with blood and peach juice. Then, pushing up the wall of the house, taking one last look at Benny and running sort of sideways down the street, he was never to be seen again.

When her Momma lost Chester, she took to the bottle again, sunk into an awful funk then before long lost her job at the mill. And soon, she was hanging out at the corner bar, until one day when she came home rip roaring drunk, with an axe in her hand, and chopped Sissie's peach tree down, and kept chopping, till there was nothing left, but firewood. And Benny would have stopped her, since he knew it was the only decent thing that he had ever done, but Benny was dead, standing up to a guy on the corner, a guy who he could have whipped, but not when the bum had a jack knife in his hand and knew how to use it.

Sissie told Gertie later, "I got smart, or so I thought, by the time that I was sixteen, and got me a wannabe pimp. I'd probably be out on that street, on that corner, with them young colored girls, and headin' for that flophouse over yonder, if you hadn't seen me, and set me up here at the Manor."

"You know, I'm doing okay. I feel like I've got a family here, with friends, and since Angie taught me manners, and how to use proper language."

"Hell, even the sex ain't bad; at least the guys are clean. I even have a few Johns coming back a couple of times a week, sorta hinting around like they may be gettin' serious, you can't tell, one of these days I might get lucky, fine the right kind of guy, maybe even get married."

The ruckus was over. The wannabe pimp was long gone, left while Sissie was talking. Now, the down-and-outers were wandering back in again in a coma like state, the way people get when fasting for too long.

Sissie got up from the window seat and started for the door, turning to Norma Jean, saying, "Damn, it's hot in here, if we're goin' downtown, I'm gonna change clothes and take a bath. I know old Louis, next door at Werner's Shop, is standing down there, leaning against the wall, just ready to pinch my ass as I go by, and right this minute, that little JoJo has got his nose stuck to the window, wantin' a peek, so I'm gonna leave the shades up, and let that little shit get an eyeful."

23

Norma Jean

Norma Jean stayed, long after Sissie left, sitting in the window seat, daydreaming. The Manor became silent, her mood darkened, tears began running down her pretty cheeks, her thoughts turned to the life she led, and to the young son downstairs, sitting on Gertie's lap, while she hummed a tune, and the little boy slept.

As she gazed through the window at the street below, on that hot summer day, when it was just barely afternoon, when the only sign of life were the stumble bums looking for a handout, or the weary sitting on the curb, shoes off, sockless feet placed flat on the pavement, head hanging between their legs, their eyes closed in a coma like sleep.

Norma Jean wasn't tough like Sissie, nor Gertie. And she hadn't led an upper class life like Angie. She didn't like the taste of whiskey, and she didn't do drugs like Angie did. She hated the way men pawed her, unlikely to fake an orgasm, Sissie who never seemed to mind.

Norma Jean had confessed her sins to Sissie before, telling the story of her young life when they began rooming together. She told her tale, almost kneeling, as if she were in a confessional,

Sissie a defrocked priest, telling it all, hoping for some sort of forgiveness, maybe a penance from Sissie to make everything all better. Norma Jean knew there was no forgiveness for her, the sin that she cherished was the baby boy, sitting on Gertie's lap.

"You know Sissie, we didn't have it bad like you. My dad had a steady job, a salesman at a hardware store. He didn't make much, but with my older brother Jason helping out, doing odd jobs in our neighborhood, we did okay."

Norma Jean added, "The little old ladies all loved Jason, and so did their granddaughters."

She sat, looking hard at Sissie, trying to make up her mind if she should continue, finally, she said, "Jason was one good looking guy, polite, and athletic with all the things that would attract the girls, but shy as a mouse." She added, "You know, I think, that at times, Dad thought he might be gay. But I knew better."

Norma Jean began crying, "Our house was on a street filled with bungalows, a mixture of blue and white collar families. I even had my own bedroom, and Jason, Mom and Dad had one too. Jason was two years older than me, and at seventeen I think that the only thing he had done was kiss a girl."

The chain of events that changed Norma Jean's life began on a warm summer day, when their Mom had gone shopping, and their Dad at work. Jason came in from mowing lawns, soaking wet with sweat, and covered with grass shavings. As he walked to the bathroom to take a shower he glanced into Norma Jean's bedroom where she lay pretending to read a magazine. All summer Norma Jean had watched as Jason made a point of showing more and more of himself when he was sure that Norma Jean was in view. That day, Jason stood in the doorway, his face red, staring straight at Norma Jean, then undressed, never taking his eyes away from her face until he was naked.

She was sure now that it was going to happen. Norma Jean,

who had never been touched, stood still as stone as her brother and her best friend stood before her, waiting.

With a silent nod of understanding, she turned and quickly undressed, keeping her back to him, afraid of how her thin, undeveloped body would look. Without a word being said, the two fell on the bed together and began touching, experimenting, fondling, more like lovers than brother and sister. Then everything happened too quickly. Jason let loose with a low groan, losing his seed as Norma Jean barely fondled him, spraying her hand with his sperm.

Jason, his face red with shame, lay quietly until Norma Jean began quivering as Jason tenderly reached between her legs, gently rubbing all the places that seemed to please her until she cried out in relief. It was a simple act, almost clinical, but it opened floodgates.

Brother and sister never spoke a word. Jason quickly went to the bathroom and shut the door while Norma Jean dressed, straightened the bed and left the house at a run, her head spinning, feeling somehow only partially fulfilled, and yet, not in the least bit guilty.

That summer seemed to fly by. Jason always had a girlfriend, and more than once, Norma Jean was sure that there was the musky smell of sex on Jason's clothing, but if he had sex with some girl, unknown to Norma Jean, she never knew, nor cared, while she ran around with boys, and girls in a pack, with other kids her own age.

Somehow the siblings became one. Jason entered Norma Jean the second time, as they lay down together, and with it came a climax so intense she screamed.

They never questioned what they were doing, whether it was right or wrong, or that it was incest, surely not in their eyes. To them it was a natural act between two curious youngsters.

The summer of awakening for the two youngsters ended,

and the affair was over, if there had been one to begin with. The Depression had deepened, the little chores that kept Jason with spending money were gone, and, without a second thought, maybe even relief, Jason left to work on a WPA Project somewhere in Utah.

The family, typical of so many others in that period, was no more or less intact, and yes, the two were brother and sister again, no longing, no lust, as if the experiment had been the most natural thing in the world.

But for Norma Jean a nightmare was just beginning. The month after Jason left she missed her period. At sixteen she knew those sort of things happened, but by the third month there was no doubt that she was pregnant.

She was a strong sensible girl, full of life, with many friends, but no one close enough to confide in. She was the type of good-looking girl, one who everyone liked, but somehow kept her distance, never snobbish, just sort of self-contained.

When her Mom began asking questions, she herself knowing what morning sickness was like, and if she was pregnant, Norma Jean refused to answer. She knew that no one, including Jason, should know whose baby she carried.

Norma Jean's father and mother were strict in their religion, no give or take in those two. To them Norma Jean was damned, her shame beginning to show more each day for all the neighbors to see. At the very least there was a wedding to be arranged, in a quiet ceremony, somewhere far away. Thus began a rough patch in Norma Jean's young life. Her parents were beside themselves.

Her mom coaxing at the beginning then demanding, "Honey, who is the boy? We didn't even know that you were that close to anyone."

And her dad raving at her, "Come on Norma Jean. I want his name. I'll see to it that he does the right thing by you."

Norma Jean became a different person, someone that her parents had never seen before. She was adamant, refusing to even acknowledge that she was pregnant, nor answer the coaxing of her mother, or the ranting of her father.

"I was lost," Norma Jean told Sissie, "There had never been a boy in my life, I had no best friend, except my brother, and he was the last person that I could confide in. For years, I had saved, hoping someday to go to college. I had run out of excuses with my parents, my belly was beginning to show, I felt shame for my family, so I took my clothes, and what little money I had saved, then left in the middle of the night."

Norma Jean spent the following year living a life of hell. She began wandering, first staying at the YWCA for a short time, changing her name when she registered.

She felt insecure, afraid that her parents might look there, not used to the language of the loud-mouthed girls from small towns, girls that she didn't connect with, no one to explain her problems to, and the rent eating up her cash.

There was one older woman at the Y, one who would drift away, then return, never in need for money, and always kind to Norma Jean. It was obvious to all that the woman was somehow involved with something not quite legit, her clothes were too high class, and one of the country girls would say, "Where in the hell does she get the money that she throws around."

Then, on a rainy night, when the lobby was almost empty, the country girls gone to the movies, or out with a boy, the woman sat on the sofa, next to Norma Jean. "Honey, I think you need somebody to talk to or am I wrong," she said. "Why don't you tell me what the problem is, maybe I can help."

Norma Jean had spent all those months, her feelings shut down, her friendship nothing but a smile, and now, here was a grown woman, with a sweet smile, offering solace.

So Norma Jean poured out her troubles, not the part about Jason, no one would ever know that secret, but the story of a good family, and a daughter gone astray. In the end she said, "So I've got no money, no family, and I'm going to have a baby."

The woman who Norma Jean never knew by name thought for a minute, then opened up saying, "Look Honey, I'll give you the name of a place. It's in a rough part of town, It's called the Manor. Go there, and ask for Gertie, and see if she will make room for you. You'll be with some good girls, and learn the proper way to entertain high-class Johns. It's not a bad life, believe me, I know. And in the meantime, get some help. A nice girl like you doesn't need to be staying here."

She added, "But first, you're going to need some help with that baby. There's a mission down on Second, a good haven for unwed mothers, it's known to be a good clean home. Go give it a try."

The woman rose tall and pretty, with a scent of expensive perfume, hugged Norma Jean, and went to her room, never to be seen by Norma Jean again. The next morning Norma Jean did as the woman advised, caught a trolley to the mission on Second. The building was tall, built in the shape of a dormitory, the exterior coated with stucco, walled in by brick, with a heavy wood plank door.

Norma Jean rang a bell on the side of the door, waited impatiently, and then rang again. When the door swung open, there stood a woman, stern faced, and large in stature, a person of a certain age, neither young nor old in appearance. With one look at Norma Jean's bloated stomach, she said, "Come on in missy, I think you're in need of some comfort," and with that, reached out a callused hand and brought her inside.

The mission was run by women who ran the place with tough rules. For the most part, they had led a hard life, and had no truck for pity; it was not a place for weaklings.

There were prayer meetings when the girls first rose, and after that breakfast, then chores to be done. The work wasn't hard, but it was tiring, and monotonous. Norma Jean's attitude toward the world hardened as her time approached. She had lied about her age, and kept a low profile around the other young women, all of them nonchalant about having a baby. They seemed to care little, knowing that it was best not to get attached, since the baby was to be left, given up for adoption.

Most of the girls had little or no education. They were tough, mostly born and raised in illiterate families, living on farms, or log cabins, homes up in the hills, far from Memphis, the type of place that grew corn for moon shining.

Most had never seen an indoor toilet, nor anything but a washtub to bathe in. They had simply been put on a bus, given a small amount of money, after some roughneck farmer boy or possibly a relative knocked them up. And if it was some kin, the Momma didn't want to know.

Those country girls were not unkind, but could hardly understand why Norma Jean was in such a state, and they would say to her, in a not unkindly voice, "Hell honey, it's just part of life. You have that baby, let these good folks here find a home for the baby, then get on with your life."

The time finally came. On a morning in spring, as a breeze, laced with the smell of honeysuckle, as it drifted through the open window, a midwife, a kind faced woman, with hands as gentle as lambskin, reached into Norma Jean, and delivered a red skinned little boy.

The woman talked to Norma Jean, explaining how it was best to give the baby up, the little boy could be raised in a good orphanage, or maybe even adopted. But Norma Jean knew that she would never let that little boy get away from her, that she would do anything to keep the two of them together.

Within a few months, Norma Jean left the mission, simply walked out with her baby, with no destination, a small amount of money, a young lady, barely past puberty, and the face of a cute fourteen year old.

She knew that the woman at the YWCA had told her where the place called the Manor was located, part of a street named Poplar, in an area called Skid Row. When she asked, half of those girls at the Mission talked about it, most seeing it as a haven, a sort of place where they could stay in the city, do what they had been doing, but get paid for it.

What Norma Jean saw when she first walked down the crumbled street, her baby in her arms, she felt dizzy. "My God," she thought, "There's nothing here but bums, and over yonder, all I see on that corner, are some young girls, some black, some white, not even as old as me." And here came a guy, his tee shirt rolled up, cigarettes stuffed in his sleeve, standing next to those girls, talking, and them looking scared. Then, the greasy haired thug turned and stared at Norma Jean, in a way that made her shudder.

Then, Norma Jean looked over there, next to that old weedy grass, and there stood a big old house, the one the woman had called the Manor, and told her about, telling her, "Honey, that's where all them high-steppers live, it'll be a safe place for you. Go there and ask for Gertie."

Then that greasy headed old boy, cigarette hanging from his lips, quit talking to the young girls, and started across the street toward Norma Jean, and, quick as a rabbit, just like that she found herself on the porch, knocking on the door of the Manor, and the door opened, and there stood Gertie, with her stump legs, and orange hair, and there was a smile on her face, gap toothed as a pumpkin at Halloween.

Thus began one of the oddest relationships on Skid Row. Gertie became a sort of surrogate mother to Norma Jean's baby.

Sissie and Angie taught her how to dress without seeming cheap, and how to cash in on her little girl looks. Norma Jean missed her family, she hated what she did, but she found that she was with good people, the kind that cared, and a safe place for her baby.

The Manor was like a Christmas tree sitting in the middle of a rutted dirt road. It always had a shine. There was warmth that came from the place, a gleam coming from the windows. The pretty ladies seemed to float, they brought lightness, and they smiled.

Hank would say, "You know, them gals is all right. It makes a man feel good just to be around them." And, he would say, after I questioned him, "I call 'em high-steppers, JoJo, because they remind me of them Tennessee walking horses, the way they throw them long, pretty, legs up in the air."

24

The High Steppers

By the time the three women had bathed, powered, perfumed, and dressed themselves in slinky outfits, wearing pumps with the highest heels available, they were ready to head downtown to their usual hangout at Hazel's. If one looked closely, the three might remind you of Broadway show girls, prancing shoulder-to-shoulder, knees kicking high with every step, taking up the entire sidewalk.

Sissie, by far the tallest, close to six feet, big boned, blonde hair hanging down to her neckline, long faced in a becoming way, was built for big men, the type she usually attracted. Like stair steps, Norma Jean was in the middle, more cute than pretty, hair bobbed around a round faced with cupid bow shaped lips, almost plumb, just the type to attract young, college boys.

Angie walked on the inside, the smallest of the three. She was a vamp with sunken cheeks, almost too thin, a constant expression of boredom on a mouth set in a grim line, with black hair that hung loose, most likely to attract a man who wanted to be dominated.

Memphis summers are hot. They pretty well stay hot all the way straight through the evening into late night. The wisdom from the old time tinners was that Southern men were naturally horny most any time, but the hotter it got, the hornier they became.

Uncle Louis would say, "JoJo, it's all in the blood. Southern men just have blood that gets them in heat quicker than Yankees." I thought it was a bunch of crap, like a lot of things Louis professed to know, but the ladies did perk up, saying business was good.

That afternoon, most all the tinners from both Werner's and Chlem's shops were back from the jobs when the three high-steppers passed, swinging their rear ends, their high heels flashing, their step high, showing a lot of leg every step of the way.

As they passed the door where Louis stood, smiling broadly, his nose in the air, sniffing like a blood hound, knowing that sweet smell of perfume, all three stopped, giving Louis a hug, and Sissie saying, "Where's that JoJo, I want to give him a kiss."

When I showed up Sissie leaned over and kissed my red cheek while the men laughed, and I thought, "Damn it, why can't people quit calling me JoJo."

I liked Sissie, even enjoyed her kidding me, but I always stared at Norma Jean. She still looked like the girl who played the homecoming queen in the matinees that I saw on Saturday afternoons. I was sure that I was in love with Norma Jean.

That afternoon was different; it seemed to fade into an uncomfortable evening, the three women sitting on their favorite stool at Hazel's trying to look their best for the high rollers, even as underarms darkened and hair wilted. The only breeze coming from an old oscillating fan that sat on the floor near the back of the bar, doing little besides swirling dust, giving a surreal mixture of cigar smoke, bar room dirt, and rot gut whiskey.

The three women were noticing fewer high rollers with money, more Johns with less, more guys on the cheap, the kind who would prefer to buy the girls drinks, then stand around and hint, maybe want a free ride, or at least one at a cut rate.

Sissie told the bozos off, then raised a hem of her already short skirt well above a stocking top, showing the garter belt, saying, "Hey Jack, look what you're missing."

Angie was different from her two friends. She was class from the get go. She was nonchalant in her approach to sex as she was to everything in life. She came from a wealthy family, had a college education, and had lived in a house like the Manor, but one that was in splendid condition, and didn't give a damn when hard times hit and the family went broke.

Angie told the world, "Hell, I've been drinking, doing drugs, and screwing since I was fifteen." She added, "Now, I get paid to do what I was doing for nothing, I got a good place to live, and I've real friends, not those phonys that I grew up with."

Angie loved Norma Jean, seeing in her all of the qualities that she had lost, the sweetness, the innocence that couldn't hide itself, no matter how hard she tried. Angie saw the distaste in Norma Jean's face when she was hit on by a well-to-do older man, even when he was a perfect gentleman, looking at Angie with such pitiful anguish, as she left the bar to cross to Frank's Hotel that Angie decided to help in her own special fashion.

Before the next visit to Hazel's, Angie introduced Norma Jean to her magic potion, known as cocaine. Just a sniff, a booster. Something to make the eyes shine. Something to make her special friend feel free of herself. Soon Norma Jean became enamored with the magic potion that Angie possessed, but Angie, feeling responsible for her special friend, only allowed her a small dose, a sniff up each nostril, before they set out, and by the time the three arrived at Hazel's an hour later Norma Jean seemed to float, a dreamy smile on her face, one that lasted the entire evening.

But Angie knew there would have to be limitations. Before the first week ended Norma Jean was in her room early one morning, saying, "Honey, that stuff makes my whole body tingle, can't you give me just a smidgen more, maybe a pinch for today."

Angie took one look, and thought to herself, "Uh-oh. We better be careful here. I've got enough trouble keeping myself straight. I ain't about to get this little girl hooked."

It was only a matter of time before Sissie saw the difference in Norma Jean, and when she did, all hell broke loose in the Manor, filled with the screaming threats of Sissie, telling Angie, "You keep this shit up, get Norma Jean in trouble, and I'll get Gertie to throw your ass out on the street."

But Gertie had seen the difference in Norma Jean before Sissie, and she sided with Angie. The three of them talked it out, and Sissie, who could see the distaste as well, agreed to leave well enough alone, that no real harm was being done, as long as Angie kept her word.

Now the threesome women were sitting, languishing might be a more appropriate way of putting it, touching up their makeup, ready for the high rollers to show up, all three having a scotch and water, weak on the scotch, the only drink that Joey, the bartender would serve them, the only drink that wasn't watered down rot gut, or piss poor beer, when the bar door opened, and in walked the tinner by the name of Billy, the one who worked for Chlem Sheet Metal.

Sissie started to laugh, saying, "Billy, what the hell are you doing in here, don't you know this place is for old geezers with money."

And that's when Billy shot back at her, "Hell Sissie, I got me some money, just as good as those old farts, and I got me a coat and tie on, and I didn't come here to see your silly ass anyway, I come to see Norma Jean."

With that Billy stood stiff as stone, staring at Norma Jean, looking tough, even though he had only one good arm, the other a withered sort of stump, yet handsome when he was cleaned up like this, the bad arm stuck in his coat pocket, giving an almost debonair look, but unable to quite pull it off.

Instead Billy fumbled his way along the bar, reaching in his pocket, and pulling out a bunch of wadded bills, handing them to Norma Jean, saying, "Miss, can I take you across the street to Frank's for a while," and, almost under his breath, adding, "I ain't gonna do nothin' to hurt you."

None of the three women knew what to say. "Don't Billy know," Sissie thought, "This place is for bankers and cotton men, and such, it sure ain't for tinners, especially ones with half an arm." Sissie told herself, "Don't Billy know that tinners and them like him always go to the Cotton Club on Beale to pick up women, or one of them little young girls, standing right around the corner from Chlem's Shop, right across the street from the flophouse?"

Norma Jean had seen Billy looking at her, as she sat on the porch of the Manor, as he came out of Chlem's Shop, then the way he stood so stiffly, staring, until she would raise a hand and wave, just a neighborly reaction, but instead of a return wave Billy would duck his head, as if embarrassed.

Now, here he was, right in front of her, a big, handsome guy, something she had never noticed before, fidgeting from one foot to the other, knowing that this was no place for him, no matter how well dressed.

"So now what," thought Norma Jean, but then fortified by that wisp of white powder, she extended her hand, and began putting on her little girl act, saying prissily, as she grabbed Billy by his helpless arm, "Come on Billy, let's find a nice room, overlooking Main, where we can have some fun."

But Billy was filled with misgivings. Here he had got himself all cleaned up and come down here to talk, just talk, to Norma Jean, not to go bedding her down, and here she was, tugging on his bad arm.

153

As the two reached the door to Frank's Billy stopped, digging his heels into the sidewalk, saying in a pleading voice, "But you don't understand Norma Jean, I just wanna talk. I told you that I didn't want to do anything to hurt you." However, by then Norma Jean had half pulled Billy through the door. Then the two of them were heading up the stairs to a room at Frank's Hotel, a special room just for Norma Jean, one that faced Main Street, after she obtained the key from a big ole fat boy. He was as unkempt as the lobby surrounding him, dressed only in an undershirt, with suspenders, holding up a belly big as a watermelon sitting on baggy pants. The guy never looked up from a *True Detective* magazine he was reading, simply passed the key over a dirty counter.

They were soon down the hall, Norma Jean leading the way, opening the door to a gaudy room, covered with bright red, flowered wall paper, a brass bed, and a picture hanging off kilter, of snow capped mountains, one that looked as if it were picked up at a starving artists sale.

She then turned to Billy, saying, in a dreamy fashion, "Here we are Billy, ain't this just what you wanted," and before Billy could say a word, Norma Jean was down to her bra and panties, her high heels kicked off, and stretched out on the almost clean sheet, ready to let Billy have a go.

But Billy, stood unmoving, his clothes still intact, looking sad, and hurt, telling Norma Jean, "Hell naw Hon, I didn't come here for a poke, all I want to do is talk with you."

Billy sat in the one chair, stuttering at first, while Norma Jean lay with her back against the wall, pulling a piece of the sheet over her nearly naked body, suddenly modest, the affect of the white powder gone, feeling insecure, like a young girl reborn.

Norma Jean listened quietly as Billy told her how much he loved her, from the minute she showed up at the Manor, the way she looked in that yellow summer dress, the way she seemed to float down the sidewalk, and the way he sometimes followed her when she left the Manor, and made her way to that empty lot a block away, filled with dead grass, yellow as a ripe banana, her little boy running in front, pushing his tricycle.

And way he stood out of sight, watching for the wannabe pimps who haunted the streets, looking for fresh meat, especially beauties like Norma Jean. How mother and child constantly touched each other for reassurance, as if they were afraid one would disappear from the other.

When he had finished everything he had to say, looking exhausted, his mouth turned down, his eyes sad, Norma Jean sat up and stared, looking at Billy with unsure eyes, tearing up, as a sadness, like an evening fog, came over her so quickly that she felt herself spinning, suddenly feeling once more, the effects of the white stuff, trying to stand, but falling back.

All of the thoughts that had been dammed up in Norma Jean's mind began flowing back. The family that was gone, never to be seen again. The shame she felt as she put on that little girl act, making the Johns feel as if they were virile, manly gentlemen. The way the men treated her, tenderly for the most part, never mean, almost, but not quite, as if she were a virgin.

Norma Jean looked at Billy, and for the first time in years thought of her brother Jason, those same soft eyes, the handsome face, the gentle timid manner, and yet, a determination that she had not seen until now.

And, she said, "Billy, you don't know one thing about me. Any way you cut it, I'm nothing but a damned whore. Forget the money, let's get out of here." And, in a voice filled with a bitterness she didn't feel, she said, "I got to get back to work, or Sissie and Angie are gonna grab a hot one. There ain't a whole lot around these days, not with this damned Depression." And, she added, "I got to make enough to pay Gertie, and feed my baby, I just ain't got time for love."

25

Norma Jean Falls For Billy

Norma Jean dressed quickly, and without a word flew out the door, afraid that if she stayed the tenderness that she was beginning to feel for Billy might bloom, the love that lay somewhere inside this young girl might show.

Billy was on her heels, pleading, "Wait Norma, let's at least talk," as he reached for her with his good arm. She flew down the rickety steps, through the lobby with its faded wallpaper, and past the dusty sofa, leaving footprints on the artificial tile floor, then out the frosted glass door, and onto Main Street.

As she stepped onto the sidewalk, Norma Jean could see Sissie across the street, standing in front of Hazel's, waving her arms frantically, pointing to Norma Jean's right. She was hollering something, and as Norma Jean turned, she could see coming toward her a guy by the name of Lefty, a thug who had followed her around for months.

Lefty was yelling, "Hey bitch, I tole you ten times, if I tole you once, if you gonna work this street, you gonna work for me."

Lefty was crazy. He was big, really big, muscled up to the point of being gorilla shaped, was a half-assed pimp, with a stable of young black girls, who he beat with a willow switch, when he was high on coke, a habit that had burned his brain, until most of the young girls hid from him, the few that were afraid to run, so covered with red welts no Johns would get near them.

Somehow, in that thick head, Lefty had come to consider Norma Jean part of his stable, his one prize, among the poor little heifers that he had beaten half to death. Now he was right there, not ten feet away, red eyes bulging out, coked up so badly that he was spinning, then doing a little tap dance, talking to Norma Jean, all the time muttering to himself.

Billy came out the door of the hotel just as Lefty reached in his pocket, came out with his flick knife, and started toward Norma Jean, saying, "You're mine bitch, you're mine."

The blade was half out of his pocket when it stuck, Lefty still screaming, "I'm gonna cut that pretty little face till you can't get fifty cents for a lay," but doing everything in slow motion, the drugs beginning to take over, having more and more effect.

Billy, seeing Lefty as he came through the lobby, had picked up an old lounge chair, stepped clear of the door and chopped Lefty across the back of his head. Everything went quiet with that one blow. Lefty went down at a funny angle as he hit the sidewalk, his head sounding like a ripe watermelon when it hit, then he lay, still as death. For just one minute, there seemed to be no movement. Billy stood with a broken chair still in his hands and Norma Jean was frozen until Sissie ran across the street and hugged her.

The fat man had come out from behind the counter at Frank's, still in his undershirt and suspenders, taking his time, wanting no part of the action, then stood, staring down for a minute, saying, "Looks like you might have kilt that ole boy. If you did, I'd say it's good riddance." Then he added, almost as an afterthought, "Looks like you owe me five dollars for that chair you broke, but we'll let her go, just to get rid of that son-of-a-bitch."

Lefty just lay there, while Norma Jean, Billy, and some

onlookers, mostly drunks, stared at the unmoving body. Soon, a group of young black girls, their bodies covered with welts, inched up to the still form, and began kicking Lefty, timidly at first, then with such venom even the drunks were appalled.

Billy was scared, sure that he had killed Lefty, but Sissie reached down and rolled his head enough to see that he was breathing, saying, "Don't worry Billy, Lefty's got a knot on his head big as a walnut, but he's alive."

When the police arrived, Abe Chlem was there, called by Sissie, standing, with an arm around Billy, greeting the cops by name, explaining how Lefty had attacked Norma Jean, and how one of his best men had protected her.

The cops grabbed Lefty by the neck and threw him into the back seat of the police car, saying, "If you're gonna be sick, let us know, you hear."

With that, it was all over but the shouting, the crowd of drunks and whores dispersed, the drunks looking for a handout, and the young black girls, dancing down the sidewalk, hugging and giggling. Norma Jean, the color returning to her face, turned to Billy, and with a sheepish grin, asked, "Do you think we might take a ride down to the park, the one by the Mississippi, and sit for a spell, I want to tell you a lot of things that you likely don't want to hear, and then Billy, if you still feel right about us, we'll take it from there."

Sissie watched as the two got into Billy's old truck, seeing tears running down Norma Jean's face, and felt a sadness, sure that she was about to lose a friend, only to be left with Gertie, her orange haired madam, but probably not for long, if she kept hanging out with that Russian son-of-a-bitch, and Angie, who day by day was becoming more of a cokehead.

Norma Jean would tell Billy the truth about her brother Jason, leaving nothing out about the incest, and make neither excuses, nor the way that she felt any guilt. And Billy would tell Norma Jean how his daddy had killed himself, and how his mama left him, just walked away, when he was a baby. Sissie smiled to herself, picturing Billy, dull as old paint, a one armed tinner, but loyal, and sweet, and tough enough if need be. And how he would talk Norma Jean into marrying him, then the two of them going to her home, where she would introduce Billy to her parents, and show the baby, who she would claim, looked just like Billy.

26

Sissie and Eudora

Sissie returned to her stool in the darkened bar, looked at Joey, the bartender, and ordered a large scotch, straight-up, no water, then gave Joey a dirty look when he raised his eyebrows, and very nearly shook his head.

Joey was a big guy, strong as a mule, hired as much for his muscle as his drink mixing abilities. He was the handsome, clean sort, rarely lost his temper, a good listener, and a close friend to Sissie. Being a friend had made Joey raise his eyebrows, since Sissie hardly ever took a drink, even with a client, a word that sounded more high class than calling the guy a John, and, as Joey could have predicted, Sissie was wobble eyed after downing half the glass of scotch.

"You know what Joey, I think I'm drunk. I just ain't used to liquor," Sissie said, "I've been thinking a lot lately, I'm sick of this life, and I'm sick of me."

Sissie sat saying no more to Joey, but feeling droopy while waiting patiently for a client, as the afternoon wore on. She felt as if she were standing outside herself, a spectator, staring at this strange woman, wondering who she was, and somehow, having a dislike for what she saw.

Hazel's was unusually quiet for a Saturday, only the three of them together, close friends, not any conversation necessary. Soon, Angie began to snore, then drifted toward the floor, gradually sliding off the stool, until Joey rounded the bar, shook her a little, giving her back a pat, and Angie, already coked out, drifted back into her own dream with a smile.

By now the well to do Johns were back at their fancy homes, with their well-dressed wives. The bums who came through the door this late in the day were moochers, most on the dole, wanting a poke on the cuff, making pests of themselves, until Joey would run them out of the place with his Louisville slugger.

Somehow Sissie knew that she had lost that touch for banter, kidding her way into bed, having fun, enjoying the feel of a man, enjoying the sex, even the old and withered, who seemed to appreciate her as a woman much more so than the younger guys who thought of themselves as studs.

As their members lay flaccid, Sissie had a way of coaxing the embarrassed old gents into a few moments of pleasure. Most of the time Sissie simply closed her eyes, drifting off into a world known only to herself, where any touch was one of enjoyment, the touch of a man inside her was an act of pure pleasure, if not for herself, then by the simple act of giving to another.

Now Sissie lay her head on the slick, cool, mahogany bar, remembering the nightmares, her Mama, and Benny, and Chester, and she whimpered as she lay in a stupor, at the memory of the loss of that wonderful peach tree, the one living thing that bore fruit, killed by her own Mother, just one more reason for the hate that she carried, that lay just beneath the surface.

Sissie raised her wobbly head, "You know what Joey, I'm gonna quit the trade. I just reached the time where I don't like myself anymore. I feel like a hunk of meat. It's gettin' so I hate the touch of a John's hands, even the nice old guys make me squirm."

Joey, was quiet for a minute, looking down to the curve in the old bar, staring at the still passed out Angie, and said, "Tell you what Sissie, if you leave, the only thing left is Angie, and I don't think she's gonna be around for long."

Then looking at her to be sure it wasn't just whiskey talking, added, "I've kinda thought for a long time that you oughta get out of the trade, this place is beginning to change for the worse, it might be a good idea for you to sober up, and go talk things over with Gertie."

Sissie sat a few minutes longer, thinking of what Joey had said, then stood, knees buckling a little, wondering how in the hell she had become so drunk on one scotch, straightened her dress, applied new lipstick, took one last look in the mirror, seeing a pretty, disheveled, half sober woman, then walked out the door. And, as she did, it was with a backward wave of a loose hand to Joey, knowing that she would probably never see him again.

As Sissie waited on the corner, the darker skinned girls, some with switch marks still on their legs, flocked around her, remembering the way she had she stood by them. And they hugged, and patted, and giggled, sure that they were free now from that son-of-a-bitching pimp, and that filthy bed in the flophouse.

Now they were ready to make their own choices, maybe save up enough money to leave, go back home, a place they never should have left, and at least, make something of themselves, maybe find a decent man and get married, have babies, do all those things that they had run away from.

Sissie hugged the young girls back, some just teenagers in hand-me-down dresses, shapeless things that had been washed far too many times with the look of old flour sacks, feeling for the first time in a long while that there may be some hope.

As Sissie stepped onto the trolley, she waved back, then sat on one of the hard wooden seats, riding toward the Manor and

Gertie, but, as the old streetcar rocked back and forth, she stared out the window, and there, across the street, stood the mission, the one where Norma Jean had spent that year having her baby.

Without a second thought Sissie pulled the clanger, and as the streetcar slowed, dropped off onto the pavement, then walked the half block back to the mission.

Sissie's first thought was, "This damned place looks just like Norma Jean described it." Old and dusty, at first sight it seemed threatening, but as Sissie came close, she could see that the harshness disappeared, and instead, she felt a sense of peace.

Sissie raised the hammered brass knocker, all the while thinking of how Norma Jean had talked with great affection, of the way she had been treated so decently during her stay.

When the thick wooden door opened, a woman of a certain age, anywhere from forty to sixty, the same woman Norma Jean had described, stood in some sort of suit, not that of a nun, nor a nurse, but surely in some sort of uniform, all brown and drab, with no adornment whatsoever.

She was a huge woman, six feet at least, broad shouldered, and grim faced, lips pressed tightly together, a strange face, but not altogether unpleasant.

Sissie stepped back, as the woman said, in a loud, gravelly voice, "Can I help you miss?"

Sissie, usually not one much for backing down, said, "Yes Ma'am, but I ain't sure how. I seem to be lost," then added, "You think I can come in for a while."

As Sissie spoke those words, in a somewhat shaky voice, and looked at the woman, larger than life, whose face had suddenly softened, transformed into one of compassion, she burst out crying, and stepped into those huge arms, and the most astounding feeling of peace passed from this stranger's body into hers.

Eudora, for that was the name Sissie remembered, and

when Sissie asked, said, "Of course, I remember Norma Jean, but it's plain to see you ain't here for the same reason."

Sissie and Eudora talked of simple things as they took a tour of the mission, which had once been an old rooming house, and had been renovated to some degree by the few women who lived and worked there.

There were usually three to four women, beaten wives, probably some of the same women who had been there when Norma Jean had her stay, ones who had escaped husbands, or bums who they lived with, the sort of men with no job, who lived on the women's paycheck, or borrowed whiskey, often taking out their frustrations by beating hell out of their women.

Some of these women might stay only a short time, then return to the hell that they fled, only to show up, months later, eyes swollen shut, cut lips, ready to stay, leave for good the monsters who beat helpless women.

Many, once they had their freedom, lasted for years, cooking decent meals in the dinky little kitchen, or scrubbing the floors, working with the girls, helping them through their pregnancies, giving them the love that they never knew when they were young.

"We take girls in every day, just like Norma Jean," Eudora said. "If they got any money to help with expenses, they hand it over, and if they don't the girls help out, doing chores, as long as they're able."

Eudora said, "When the baby comes, we got a good mid-wife. She's the same one who took care of Norma Jean, when her time came, an ole gal from the hills. She's got an awful twang, so bad I can hardly understand her, but she's clean, even though she don't smell real good, and she ain't lost a little one yet."

Eudora went on, "Then, when the Mother is fit, and the baby is healthy, we give them a choice. They can leave with the baby, or go off on their own, and we'll take care of the little one."

And she added, "We got a deal with that new government program that helps place these kind of girls, but you might as well know, most of them girls didn't want that baby to begin with, and then on some morning, she'll just be gone, leaving those little tykes with us, then, next thing you know," she said, "they'll be back on a corner until they get in such bad shape they end up in one of them cribs in the whorehouses downtown on Mulberry Street."

"I don't know how many babies we got," Eudora said, "but it's more than we can care for, but now, luckily, we may have found a place out a ways, a Catholic orphanage, by the name of Saint Peters. It's run by a group of nuns, and they seem real nice. I'm gonna meet with 'em next week, and if you want, you might tag along. I ain't very good at talkin' to religious kind of folks."

With that, Eudora stopped, looking embarrassed, her face turning a bright red, suddenly realizing that she was letting out her woes to a perfect stranger.

Eudora, in her deep southern drawl, all the while, had been coaxing Sissie into talking about herself, and why she had come to her mission.

As they walked Sissie let everything out, tears running down her cheeks as she spoke of her life before Skid Row, and how she was ready to leave everything behind, and start over.

Sissie spoke of the men she had been with, the way their touch had made her feel, the comfort from their body, but now, a longing to be apart from that life, and do something good, to help these young girls through their troubles and, maybe, in doing so make the dark thoughts that lived in her mind disappear.

From that day, Sissie and Eudora became a team. Surprisingly, they fit like a glove. Eudora had never been married. Very likely she had never dated. She kept her personal life to herself, clamming up when one of the do-gooders brought up personal things, began quizzing her, while Sissie opened up to all, wanting the women to know what it was like to be on the street, not bashful, telling the good, and the bad.

At times she used language even Eudora had never heard, until those girls from the hills, or the hovels near the river, where they had been raped by their cousins, or sometimes their daddy, learned to love Sissie and, as Eudora grew older and the aches with age began to take their toll, Sissie began taking command with the same toughness that Eudora had used but, if one gazed closely, there was always a smile of peace on her face. And Sissie was sweet to the girls, most of them almost kids. She held them in her arms, giving them the love she that she missed as a child.

Then, on a spring day, when the rain the evening before had moistened the soil, Sissie walked away from the mission, then returned a few hours later with a large hauling truck driven by a hearty looking man, Sissie riding shotgun. She jumped out and ran into the room where all the women were working and announced to Eudora, "Honey, I got a bunch of saplings outside. I need some help in planting them."

And soon, the girls giggling as they worked, planted a small orchard of peach trees smack in the middle of the courtyard, ones that would grow large and healthy as the girls cared for them, and bear fruit for the years to come.

Sissie, who selected which women would join the mission and spend their lives there, had to be careful, some having been treated so badly by their husbands or live-ins that they hated all men, a bitterness that carried over into the young girls. But Sissie surprised herself, never realizing that she was good at balancing the tough, almost unmanageable with the very vulnerable.

After Sissie had been at the mission for a year, and as she and Eudora were beginning to act toward each other as if they were an old married couple, she began to feel closed in, incomplete in ways that she couldn't fathom, finally deciding to open herself, wondering if she had lost the inner strength to touch the friends that she had left behind.

She had always felt badly for leaving Angie sitting on a bar stool at Hazel's, that glazed look on her face and, even though afraid of what she might find, Sissie left the mission late one afternoon, and caught the street car down Main to Hazel's. When she walked in the door, the smell of cheap booze, beer, and smoke almost made her too dizzy to stand, but also brought back memories, not all of them unpleasant.

The bartender was a tall, slim, slumped over sort, with a cheap, ill fitting wig, and a grim expression, but when Sissie asked if Joey was on duty, the guy answered, in an unusually polite voice, "Don't know him miss, I only been working here a couple of weeks."

As Sissie looked around the bar, it seemed seedier than she remembered, and the few patrons seemed to be the type who would fit in more suitably at the Red Rose. When she asked about the whereabouts of Joey or Angie, the few who didn't answer with a blank stare, simply shook their heads, most saying, "Ain't never heard of them."

Sissie began to feel desperate, as she walked out the door, where she stood on the corner, and noticed one of the young black girls, the one by the name of May, one of the bunch who had switch marks, one of the kids, from months before, who had giggled, as they kicked hell out the pimp. And when she waved, the young girl saw her and whopped, then ran across the street to give Sissie a hug.

"Where you been girl, we ain't see you in a coon's age," the kid said, and when Sissie told May that she was out of the racket, May said, "Might be a good thing, this corner's gone to hell in a hand basket, nothing but bums and guys on the dole around here now. A gal can't make a living even if she worked till midnight."

Then Sissie asked what happened to Joey and Angie, and as

she did May's face darkened. "Sissie, I hate to tell you, but that's part of the mess. Joey got run off by the son-of-a-bitch that bought the place, he was just too straight, the way he kept the riff raff out, wouldn't water down the drinks, and treated people fair. Now they got bums and pimps in there, and gals that'll turn a trick for a quarter."

May added, "When Joey got fired, Angie lost the only friend she had, 'cept for you, then she got into that coke so bad, she lost all her senses. Last I heard, she was laying up in a crib in one of them whorehouses over on Mulberry, and she ain't got hardly any customers, cause she don't take care of herself."

Sissie thanked May, then, half crazy, ran the few blocks to a dirty, shotgun house on Mulberry, went up the rickety old steps, banged on the door, and when no one answered, walked through. As Sissie entered, directly in front of her sat an old man, drunk, his head on a table, sound asleep, a wet spot on the floor, where he had wet himself, and behind the table a long hall, paint peeling from the mottled plastered walls, with eight or ten, warped doors, all closed. Without slowing, Sissie sidestepped the old man, and walked down the hall, banging on closed doors as she did, hollering for Angie. Finally a girl, one who looked to be about fifteen, with dirty hair, and crooked teeth, cracked a door, and pointed to the room across the hall.

Sissie knocked, then threw the door open, and entered a room, dark as midnight. Under a filthy spread lay a lump, and when she pulled the cloth away Sissie knew, before she knelt to hold her, that she had lost her best friend. Angie lay in a fetal position, curled up, with a slight frown, a quizzical expression on her thin face, as if she questioned where she was, and how she had gotten there.

Sissie never forgave herself for deserting Angie. She didn't smile as much after Angie died, and was much stricter with the girls. From that day forward, the use of drink or drugs, even weed, was reason enough to be banned by the mission.

In time, the dullness of running the mission made Sissie edgy; an anxious feeling seemed to rest on her like an anvil. She could see the years ahead, doing good work with the young, but she felt less useful. She and Eudora had put things in their proper place, and the home almost ran itself.

Sissie knew that it was time to move on, to try to lift the weight of guilt that lay on her like a too heavy blanket. There was no guilt about the men she had bedded, that was only an afterthought, but surely there was so much more to be done, some good to satisfy her thirst for atonement. And, without another thought, Sissie caught the next trolley going in the direction of Skid Row.

27

Skid Row Loses A Good Man

Louis died on the sort of day that he loved, a warm day but not too warm, when he could stand, leaning against the open doorway, cigarette in hand, his blind eyes fluttering, feeling the warmth of the sun, the down-and-outers, winos, bums greeting him with a "hi," as they passed by, as if he were an old friend.

A damned fool doctor, one of my uncle's best friends during the glory days when they both were rounders, had misdiagnosed a ruptured appendix, and by the time a competent doctor discovered the mistake, the poison had done its work. His death seemed to make the dreary street even darker. My dad came from the hospital, stopped the Plymouth in front of the shop, then sat, his head resting on the steering wheel, his eyes closed for the longest time, before slowly opening the car door, moving like an old man, and entered the shop while I stood with Werner's men, Dad's face telling us the tragic news, even before he spoke. Word had already spread up and down Skid Row and a crowd had gathered in front of the Werner shop while we stood in a stupor in the little office.

I could hear their chatter from the sidewalk, "He was a cussed ole son-of-a-bitch," one would say. "Yeah he was that, but always good for a tap, or a meal," another would answer. "And did you see the way he always had a smile on his face," came a voice from the rear. And so it went until each had taken his turn, praising Louis, or cussing him, but all remembering.

On the first day when Dad reluctantly re-opened the shop, knowing that a death didn't stop a building from needing metal work, I had driven the Plymouth, a quiet drive, no yelling from my dad, just me at the wheel, and Dad sitting, slumped forward. I noticed for the first time the gray hair and the double chin with stray whiskers where he had missed with the razor, and the way he had seemingly aged overnight.

We were both going to miss my uncle, just as the street people, but in our own fashion. No more advice to me about girls, and the parts of them that were off limits, or, at least to be approached with caution.

And for Dad the hollering on the ride to and from work, and the unwanted advice, the proper way to bullshit the contractors, how to wheedle a project away from the competition.

Louis's death changed my father, made him less a part of the gang, more like the boss, moving him more apart than in the past. He began calling the men by their proper names, rather than nicknames, names such as Do-Right, and Black Robert, or Pear, one of the few things that he took great pleasure in. Dad had always been more serious in his approach to work than Louis, having dropped out of school in the eighth grade, while my uncle continued through high school and received his diploma.

As I grew into manhood, I came to realize that my dad was just plain scared, and always had been. With the loss of Louis, he was losing more than a brother; he was also losing a mentor.

The tinners began to talk, whining a little, as they sipped from a pint of Lem Motlow, while riding back to the shop, after I had picked them up in the old truck. "JoJo, your daddy's changed, our shop ain't what it used to be, you know. It was kinda like a family, now it's all business with him. It just ain't the same anymore."

On a day in June when the weather had turned from warm to hot almost overnight as it was wont to do in Memphis and I was looking at a set of plans, sweat dripping off my brow, then running down my arms, making wet spots on the blueprints, my mind swirling as I tried to estimate a job, unsure of myself, wondering what all the lines and figures meant, an odor drifted into the hot little office, a sweet smell, not the cheap toilet water used by the women on the row. This was a decent perfume, and I knew, before I raised my head, my friend Sissie had come to call.

Before I knew it Sissie was in my arms, hugging me, and she was saying, with eyes widened in surprise, "My God, JoJo, look at you, you're all grown up on me. If I want to give you a kiss, I'll have to get on my toes." And she did just that, a long, lingering, intoxicating kiss.

Sissie and I talked for the longest time, first one, then the other. She was devastated when I told her of Louis's death, saying, "Remember JoJo, how my buddy would stick his nose out like a bloodhound when I passed, and always pat me on the ass. My how I'll miss that old guy."

She looked across the street, and said, "Well, we still got Jew Bill. Hell, it must be ninety-five in that sun, and the ole man's sound asleep, layin' back in that cane backed chair. And look at that, he's finally got a telephone sittin' next to his chair. At least he won't miss any calls, that is, if they get any."

Sissie turned to the corner and asked, "Is that the same kids, JoJo?" And there were the young black girls, mirror images of ones from a year before, still giggling, still flirting, still waving at passersby, trying to drum up business, and, just in case, over yonder across the street stood the flophouse, paint peeling worse than ever, the same haggard looking bums sitting in the rocking chairs and old divans, beer bottles in their dirty hands.

Sissie's shoulder's sagged as she saw the Manor next door, for it was now battened down, the windows covered with planks, the columns caving in, the house ready to fall in on itself.

As Sissie stared at the Manor, she looked as if she might tear up, and then stared out onto the street, and she said as she walked away, "I'll be back in a minute." And she walked among the down-and-outers, some sitting on the curbside, others scrunched against the dusty walls, and with the smell of the street, and the unwashed people, with glazed eyes, it was all just too much, and Sissie began to cry.

As I watched, she went from one to the other, sitting on the curb, holding them, hugging some, saying words I couldn't hear, I felt that same damned stomachache coming on, the one that gave me a pain, one that was becoming a frequent visitor.

I still had the shop to myself, Dad off seeing a contractor, and the few men we employed, working on a roof somewhere, so I knew that I had Sissie to myself, still remembering that kiss.

I went to the ice cooler, got us both a cold drink, and told Sissie what had happened to me, about her friends, and what was going to happen to Skid Row.

"I'm full time now Sissie," I said, "I graduated from the Brothers last year and I'm going steady with a girl. I betcha we'll be getting married before too long, and I guess I'll end up in the sheet metal business, what with the money being so scarce I can't afford college."

Sissie smiled, always the optimist, "That's okay JoJo. I know you, it's a good trade, and this can be a good business. Besides, this damned Depression won't last forever."

Then, getting fidgety, acting as if she wanted to change a sore subject, she looked across the street, and asked, "What happened to Gertie, that shop's a mess." Crow's Shoe Shop was deserted now, doors and windows wide open, the inside covered in dust, and scrap paper, and piss, and rat droppings.

And I told Sissie what I had heard from Billy, that Norma Jean had received a letter from Gertie. She told Norma Jean, written in beautiful script, "Honey, Crow and me done got ourselves in a awful mess. We got out here to California and Crow found a Mexican, name of Chavez, and this Chavez was tryin' to start up a fruit pickers union. Well, some farmers come in one night, with sticks, and torches, burned the tents down, and cracked heads, Crow's included. Now Crow's gonna be in jail for a while, incitin' a riot, they said, although, the only thing he did was pitch a few of them fools in the bog, and halfway drowned one or two of 'em.

"I reckon I ain't got much choice but to start up another little house. There's a nice, pretty yellow place, sittin' behind a honky-tonk, way back in the fields, and I already lined up four or five girls, with a bunch more beggin' to be tried out."

But, since then Billy had no more information, except to tell everyone that the baby looked more like him every day. As Sissie and I talked, Dad drove up, and, from the lively way he jumped out of the car, I figured he and the contractor had probably had a nip or two, and maybe he had landed a job, maybe a decent sized one.

As Dad hustled into the shop, he looked at Sissie, and said, "Honey, you seem fine; I reckon the world's been treating you right." And before I could stop him, Dad said, "JoJo, did you tell Sissie what's goin' on down here."

And with that, Dad told Sissie what had developed.

"Look Sissie, I ain't suppose to say anything yet, but some guys dressed in suits and ties come by. They said they represented something called the Federal Housing Authority, and they been talking to all the shop owners. They were here at the shop, talking to JoJo and me just yesterday. It looks like they're gonna buy us all out."

Then Dad being Dad frowned. He never could believe

anything good was going to happen. "They got an offer on the table, pretty well one we can't turn down." He continued, "When they finish, this whole area will be redone with a wider street and nice shops, you know, when you think about it, it ain't all bad. With things getting better and work coming in, maybe it's time for a change."

As he finished his say, Sissie simply stared, then pointed to the street outside.

"What the hell's gonna happen to them poor fools out there if the street is gone, Mister Joe? We can't let them end up in a gutter somewhere or down by the river living in a cardboard box."

The word was out. The Federal Agency had spoken, and even someone with as much pull as Abe Chlem couldn't stop what the City Fathers considered progress. Up and down Skid Row there was a feeling of apprehension. Lord knows where the word came from, but it had spread like a flame in a windy forest. The city was going to widen Poplar Avenue and in doing so tear down Skid Row. And the down-and-outers and bums, even the Sterno sniffers who didn't know night from day, were becoming jittery wondering, "What are we going to do, where do we go?"

But all the shop owners knew. The date and the time had been set. The contracts had been signed, and within a few days Skid Row was to be vacated, and torn down.

28

The Paddy Wagons And Cops—The Doom Of Skid Row

One of the stew heads raised his head, and peaked over the bushes where he had spent half of the night pulling twigs over his body, trying to stay warm. When he saw where the racket was coming from, he leaned over and punched Jake, a fellow wino, lying spread-eagle on the wet grass, saying, "What the hell do you think them things are, Jake? They look like some kinda tanks."

It was still early, and what the stew head saw was a number of paddy wagons, square, boxlike, affairs, coming out of a low fog, pushing aside the grey mist hanging over Poplar.

As the wagons passed down the street, the stew heads could see two cops, caps pulled down on their foreheads, staring ahead, young looking fellas, their lips as straight as a number two pencil. Two of the wagons took position to block off Skid Row, one on each end, while the others stopped in the middle of the old street. As the two watched, the driver and his partner climbed down from the cab, then went to the rear, and opened a double, heavy duty screen, one that would afford air, but strong enough to prevent any thought of escape.

As the screen opened, two more policemen crawled out, not

with helmet and batons, as if this were some sort of raid, but with obvious reluctance, one of those painful duties, the dirty part of their job. The police met in the middle of the street, then after a conference, began to spread out, going from door to door, searching until every bum, wino, and just plain poor folk, were located, then with obvious reluctance, loaded them into each wagon.

Dad stood with me at his side in front of the Werner Shop as every tinner we employed stood, leaning against the block wall, grim faced, and white as stone, some quivering with rage.

Hank, Cal, Charley, Black Robert, Grinder, they all said the same thing. Hank said it best, "I ain't never seen anything like it JoJo. Them police are everywhere. Look at 'em, crawling under the Manor next door, scrounging in that filth in the back of Crow's shop. Hell, they're even dragging bums off the porch over at the flophouse."

Then Charley said, "I'll give 'em credit, them cops. They're just as gentle as could be, they look like they hate the damned job that they were doin' as much as we do watching it."

Charley added, "I swear JoJo. I heard that they're all young recruits. Abe said the older cops refused to come down here. Damned if it don't look like some of them kids got tears runnin' down their cheeks."

Across the street Abe Chlem's men were more agitated, Abe was right in front, his back to the street, talking to his men, trying to keep order, but once in a while, one or two of the tinners stepped off the pavement, ready to stop the round-up, until a few of the level headed ones grabbed their arms, and brought them back on the sidewalk.

Mostly, there was a deadly sort of silence. Only once in a while, a small whimpering sound coming from some poor slob, hung over, and hungry, shaking so badly it took two people to lift him into the paddy wagon.

Dad was terribly upset, and my old stomach ache was back with a vengeance. All of the men from Werner's shop, and the bulk of Chlem's had gone, saying, "Shit on this, I ain't gonna work today. I might just go on a bender for a week."

I knew, just as Dad had known, that the street was going to be torn up, but, like him, I never considered that the people would have to leave. I said to my dad, "You know, I somehow felt that the people would just sort of be here forever. They're almost kinfolk."

Skid Row became as quiet as a graveyard. All the shopkeepers, the bystanders, who stood silently by, were gone. Dad looked across at Abe, then the two old friends met in the middle of Poplar, and shook hands, Abe patting Dad on the back, then, on impulse, the chubby little guy reached up and gave Dad a hug. When he returned, I was waiting, as my dad closed the office door, and without a word being said the two of us drove home in complete silence.

A few days later Abe came into the office, sat down with Dad and me, explaining the outcome of that awful morning. It seemed that the parade of paddy wagons headed down the main highway, people on each side of the road, having heard the rumor long in advance, stood yelling, cussing, some throwing rocks, while the young cops, who drove with eyes straight ahead, until it reached the Mississippi state line, a distance of only a few miles from the Memphis city limits, and there they stopped at a small country town.

No one had known the destination so what happened next must have made the few folks up and about so early rub their eyes in wonder. The screen doors on the rear of the paddy wagons swung open, and out crawled the poorest looking bunch of human beings that they had ever seen.

As the men stepped down, a policeman handed each a sum of money, considerably more than the city had allocated, extra money pitched in by every man on the police force. And their ample bundles of clothes, good stuff, heavy and warm, packages of food, bought from money pitched in from the tinners and shop owners. And, here and there was a bottle of Jim Beam, compliments of Abe Chlem.

The young recruits weren't tough enough yet. As they got back in the paddy wagons and left the poor folks behind, the street folk were reaching for them, giving the young'uns a pat on the back and a hug, hell, even shed a few tears. The paddy wagons turned tail; the young recruits speeding off as fast as the old crates would go, eyes forward, never looking back, for some reason, ashamed of themselves, maybe even a little scared.

The street people stood in a clump, plunked down right in the middle of a cotton field. To one side, just a block or two away there was a train track, an engine; sitting idle, smoke drifting from the stack as it took on water. And over there, off in the distance, directly in front was a small town, containing the usual square, with a clapboard court house, white in color, and a building, surely a Baptist church. Then, when they turned, far away in the distance, were the lights of Memphis, spread off as far as the eye could see.

As the mass began to move, and mingle, when a few of the diehards had consumed a nip of ole Jim, things began to take shape. First, a goodly number who had come to Memphis saddled in a boxcar, took off at a fast clip, lace-less shoes flapping on the dirt, raising their legs to clear the cotton rows, reminding one of circus clowns as they headed for the steam engine, ready for a different place, maybe some clean air, gonna catch a ride before the engine got its fill of water.

Then a man from the little village came toward the bunch, shotgun in hand, but hanging at his side, surely not a sheriff. The burg was too small for that. He was a stout sort with white whiskers, dressed in dirty overalls, not a hell of a lot better looking than the shoddy bunch facing him.

In a voice that sounded like he was used to coaxing mules, he said, "Ya'll look like you're cold. I figure you're the same bunch we already heard that damned city was gonna dump down here." He added, "We got a plenty of land, and nobody to work it, damned young'uns done run off. If ya'll wanna stay, come on with me, and we'll see what we can do."

What was left were a few diehards, just a few half crazy stumblebums, staring at each other, holding tight that bundle of clothes, and that pint of Jim Beam, then, all turned as one, heading for Memphis, and another Skid Row.

29

The Walls Came Tumbling Down

They appeared just as the light crossed the roofs of the dilapidated old buildings. It was cold that day, really cold, with a heavy fog covering the top of the parapet walls of Skid Row, a feeling of snow in the air.

The two bulldozers that sat at the top of the hill began to inch forward, their metal tracks making a clanging racket, the noise echoing off the walls. They were as large as Sherman tanks, with exhaust pipes extending into the haze, belching black smoke, reminding one of some prehistoric monsters.

Behind each of the dozers sat a crane, the boom extending far above the buildings, cables hanging down, a huge wrecking ball attached, ready to crush the old buildings into a mass of rubble. The dozen or so dump trucks were scattered like pieces of an unfinished jigsaw puzzle, engines running, heaters on, most of the drivers with heads laid back, half asleep, waiting their turn, ready to gobble up the debris.

Dad and I stood leaning against the cold concrete of the shop wall, hands in our pockets, stomping our feet, trying to stay warm. A few of Werner's men, a grim faced Hank, and Charley, and Grinder on crutches from a fall some weeks before when he fell through a hole in the roof of a building, too hung over to notice the opening.

Then Hank had turned to me, saying, "Colder than a witches tit, ain't it JoJo? Probably gonna snow today."

We looked across the way as Abe Chlem came out of the door to his shop, Jew Bill and Billy following behind, then solemnly closed and locked the door, as if it was the natural thing to do, just leaving for a little while.

Abe hesitated, seemingly unsure of what the next course of action should be, his shoulders slumped as the three of them walked into the center of Skid Row.

When I stole a look at my father his face was filled with sorrow, the lines deepened on his ruddy cheeks, as he stepped off the curb, and walked toward Abe and his men, with Werner's tinners close behind.

As we gathered together, my dad with his arm around Abe, and the men spread out in a row on that chopped up old tarmac, Sissie appeared out of nowhere to give Dad and Abe a hug, then a quick kiss for me, before standing between the two bosses.

It must have been a sorry looking sight, a couple of bosses, a bunch of tinners, an ex-high stepper who was going to help run a new mission, and a kid who had grown from a boy to manhood, and now was a part of the whole thing.

The dozers were beginning to rev their engines. The tinners were ready to bolt, nodding their heads in agreement, pointing toward the Red Rose, just get the hell out that place, and go for the first drink of the day.

Sissie and Billy were talking about Norma Jean, and Sissie about her job at the mission, while Dad and Abe spoke of their new shops in a nice business district.

And I stood aside, watching the tinners, so anxious to leave before the destruction began. Then the four of us were bunched together, almost in a panic, at the racket from the dozers as they moved forward.

Soon, there was the thud of the wrecking ball as it tore a gaping hole through the wall of the first shop, then dust flew like a small tornado as the walls fell into themselves.

Just for a moment there was an echo, then complete silence, and with that silence an eerie feeling passed over me. I looked up, and there, sprouting from a mortar joint high in a building across the way, reaching for the sky, was a fresh sapling, bright green in color, with new leaves, so full of life, but with no place to go. As I gazed upward the huge ball crashed into the brick wall, dislodging the small sapling, throwing it to the pavement below.

In an instant Sissie had rushed to the middle of the rubble, dug deeply into the dust, and wrapped the young tree in her arms, then running back to me, saying, "Here, JoJo, now you'll have something to take with you from Skid Row."

I followed my dad and our friends off the street, never looking back. A terrible sadness engulfed me and I knew that I would plant that sapling in the yard of the new shop and as it grew it would remind me of the people who drank too much booze, had too little money, suffered through that awful Depression, and yet somehow kept their compassion and dignity.

LaVergne, TN USA
17 March 2011
220586LV00007B/121/P